THE RAVENS

D0833089

JACKIE JACOBI

Black Rose Writing | Texas

First printing

ISBN: 978-1-68513-032-9
PUBLISHED BY BLACK ROSE WRITING
www.blackrosewriting.com

Printed in the United States of America
Suggested Retail Price (SRP) $19.95

The Ravens is printed in Book Antiqua

*As a planet-friendly publisher, Black Rose Writing does its best to eliminate unnecessary waste to reduce paper usage and energy costs, while never compromising the reading experience. As a result, the final word count vs. page count may not meet common expectations.

For Kait and Ian: my everyday magic.

THE
RAVENS

CHARLEY

Raine High is on fire. It's lit from the back by the rising sun, the roof shining like embers, glowing, brilliant, electric.

"Look at that," I say to Brynn. "It's us. We did that."

"Probably," Brynn says, and then trips over a crack on the school's walkway. She doesn't fall, but the bag with the packages she's carrying for me crashes to the ground. "Oh, my God. Did these break? Are they fragile?"

They are, but I won't tell her that and send her spiraling down, down, a dark hole, not today, not this morning, when the Ravens have somehow harnessed the morning star, when the sun winks at me, *hello, Charley, good morning.*

I gather up the bag with the Ravens' presents. Nothing's rattling around, so I think they're okay. Dad holds the double doors open for us way up ahead, the doors so large, so cumbersome, a gateway, a rite of passage.

"Come on, ladies," he calls out. "Plenty of time to chat at school."

I take off, running toward Dad; he calls me and I charge, can't help it, never could.

"Charley, wait!"

But I don't wait, can't wait, not with the school's door open so wide, Dad lingering there, greeting us. I can't wait when Joss is already in the locker room by herself, thank God, Mei and Chloe gone, banished from the Ravens for good.

"Slow down!" Dad says when I get to the door, out of breath, hot, ready to rip off my coat even though it's December, even though the wind has already taken the leaves down, the colors: red, orange, yellow, first swirling and billowing, and then swept into piles, raked, bagged, discarded, the trees finally naked, the sun snaking through them and creating long shadows on the walk.

"Didn't you just say to hurry? Make up your mind, sir."

He laughs. It's a smart, witty laugh, like one of those cartoon owls who wears black glasses and a graduation cap. His coat is unbuttoned, and he's wearing his infamous tie, the one the skein talks about behind his back, with the pictures of once-banned books all over it. I have the tie memorized, but still; it astounds me, the kinds of books kids weren't allowed to read once.

"*The Catcher in the Rye*? Really?" I say, while we wait for Brynn.

"Well, the language, for one."

"Like the people who banned it didn't use that language in front of their kids, anyway. Bunch of phonies."

"Phonies?"

"Like Holden would have said. In *Catcher*."

"Clever."

Brynn catches up to us. Panting, quiet, her eyes on the ground. She's so awkward, so shy, except for that shock of her one white streak, a burst of lightning in her otherwise brown ponytail.

"You're going to come visit me soon, right, Brynn?" Dad says. "About that essay."

"Uh-huh."

"Good."

They're friends, Dad and Brynn. He knows how to draw her out, draw her gently forward, a slow turtle peeking out from its shell. *She's just young*, he says. And of course, of course, she's the same age as me and Joss, but there's an immaturity there, a lack of confidence, a shyness that keeps her small. Dad's a gifted teacher like that; he sees people. Everyone says it. Even when the rumors started, Mei and Chloe would throw that in. *It's extra awful, because he's such a good teacher.* But I don't want to think about them, never really, but most of all not right now, not when just outside these doors it's so beautiful, the leaves of the weeping willows dipping low, yellow now, the last leaves hanging on before we're blasted with snow and ice.

"Just you and me, tonight, for dinner," Dad says. "Mom's on overnight."

"Thai?"

"You got it." He puts his hand on my shoulder and a hand on Brynn's back. "Have a good day. Both of you."

And then he's gone, moving along the halls, whistling, heading toward his homeroom, where he'll be surrounded by stacks of *Macbeth* essays and rubber banded green and violet pens.

"I like your boots," Brynn says, really quietly.

"Thank you!"

"Thanks," she says back, but then I guess she realizes that makes no sense and she blushes, deep pink, her eyes down and down and always down.

But that's okay. Even if I can't make her feel completely comfortable, haven't yet figured out how to be the best friend I can be to her, it will still be a good day, with a present and a speech for her and Joss, the true Ravens, the ones who aren't traitors. And it will be a good night, too. Extra spicy Thai food, no Mom, just Dad and me, talking about banned things, like books, like witches, my sisters, burned in long ago fires whose embers burned bright, bright, like the sun this morning, winking, dazzling, *good morning, Charley.*

"They're new," I add.

Combat boots, lime green socks, so many colors; why do they think witches only wear black? Why would we, when there are so many earthly shades to choose from, glorious and bright, butterflies, snowy owls, burning orange foxes, clear water crashing over golden sand, seashells, smooth and rough, their imprints there and then washed away, transient, gone.

I take Brynn's arm and pull her toward the locker room.

"You're in a good mood, Charley, considering."

But why wouldn't I be? Considering what?

It's all so fantastic: The Ravens and their presents and our winter picnic day and me and Dad, the rumors about him squashed, the rumors just lies, the winter, the coming winter so majestic, with its fallen leaves and first freeze and with the willows just outside, gasping, grasping, holding on and holding on, beautiful.

BRYNN

We need to keep our voices low.

It's not that I'm not excited; I am, but I can already hear the skein girls climbing onto the risers in the gym. If they hear Charley talking about The Ravens, junior year will be over for us before winter break even begins.

"This is the year we'll be loud and proud!" Charley stands way above us on the locker room bench with her feather raised in the air like a flag. "This is the year we rise!"

Two identically wrapped presents sit on the bench, right next to Charley's feet. She's wearing combat boots today, with neon green socks poking from the fake leather. I'd never wear anything like that. I mean, I truly never *ever* would. My shoes are boring and my socks are grey and today I'm even more of a faker than usual, because right next to Mommy's headscarf, I have a secret essay hiding out in my backpack. My English teacher, my favorite teacher of all time, Charley's dad, had written *Plagiarism* — *see me*, in a green ink that's almost as bright as Charley's socks.

She leans down and hands Joss and me our presents.

Joss slowly opens the wrapping paper. She's become a master of showing off her Very Dramatic Ravens Boredom (spelled with all caps, Charley says) since this summer. But still, I guess no one, not even Joss, can ignore a present. She carefully slices through the tape with her thumbnail and finally pulls out a slick silver box. She holds it up to the light and we read the inscription together.

The Ravens. The Empaths. The Girls Who Feel Too Much.

They're not broken.

"For your feathers! So they stop getting crinkled." Charley's so giddy she looks like she'd swallowed six candy sugar sticks on top of a gallon of caffeine for breakfast. She's all in, all the time, carried away on a current of adventure that she gets from all the books she's read. The River Charley.

"Who are we?"

"The Ravens!" I scream whisper. I hope she knows that what I feel is loud, even if the way I say it is quiet.

I unzip the front pouch of my backpack and rummage around until I find my feather. It's definitely gotten crumpled from being shoved in there every single day for the last year. Joss stares at the air, pretending she doesn't see us waving the plumes around. "I thought we were just going to be regular friends this year," she says.

"You know why we can't. You know why we can't." Charley points her feather at Joss like a sword. "Remember our code."

"It's getting really embarrassing."

Joss's dating a boy. It's not allowed. Not in the fine print, anyway, but Charley had finally given in this summer, right around the time our now ex-Ravens, Mei and Chloe, had started those rumors about Charley's dad.

"But this is the year we rise!" Charley's red hair is pulled back into a sweeping messy bun so her face is bare and spectacular like a comet about to explode across the sky, but I'm sure it upsets her when Joss bashes the Ravens.

"This is the year we change the world!"

"That's nice," Joss says. "But — how?"

The word *how* hangs in the air for a second. Charley doesn't seem to have an answer. Obviously, very obviously, *I* don't have an answer.

"Now that there are only three of us, three of us who actually care and actually belong in the Ravens, we'll be able to make some actual changes around here."

"Mei and Chloe belonged… you just —"

"If you want to talk about this, you can go hang out with them instead."

"I'd be happy to hang out with Mei and Chloe. I'm not the one who banished them."

I hate it when they fight. *One, Two, Three, Four*, I count. *Your generalized anxiety disorder does not define you*, Daddy always says, before I yell at him that I'm not one of his clients and that he needs to stop therapying me.

Luckily, this time, it's over before Charley and Joss really start getting into it.

"Bring your new boxes to the duck pond after school. We'll do a ritual for Mrs. McLaughlin's scan."

"I'm going to Malik's after school."

"*Again*?"

"Yes?"

"But this is for Mrs. McLaughlin!'

"When's your mom's scan again, Brynn?" Joss asks.

"Next Friday."

"It'll be fine," Joss says. "I know it'll come out great. Don't worry."

"Then you'll be there? You'll meet us at the pond?" Charley says.

"I — after Malik's? Does that work?"

"Sure! It'll be even darker then." The River Charley flows again. "Don't get panicky about any of this, Brynn. We've got you."

Don't. Get. Panicky. It's so hard not to. But: *These are your friends*; I say to myself for the fifty-thousandth time. *You have friends now. Thank you,*

God, for my friends. I don't know how I would have gotten through Mommy's chemo without The Ravens.

Though: *Thank you, God?* That's just one of the many prayers I want to shed, like my cousin's snake's skin. Because what would Father Dooley think of these rituals? What would Sister Rose say?

But truly, there's no time to worry now, no time to panic, because the bell rings and we need to get out of here before Mrs. Miller takes attendance.

"We have to go," Charley says. "On three."

"One," I put my hand, which is still holding the feather, straight out in front.

"Two," Charley touches her feather to mine.

Joss's eyes are basically rolled up to her forehead, but she puts her empty hand out next to ours, anyway. "Three."

"May the spirit of the Ravens be with you today."

And also with you, I say, but just in my mind.

We hold there for a few seconds. It's like we're taking a picture, but we don't actually take one. No selfies. That's a Raven agreement in large print.

"Four more weeks till winter break," Charley says. "You ready?"

Charley and I raise our feathers into the air. Joss raises her empty hand.

•   •   •

In the auditorium, the skein is buzzing.

Charley says the other girls at our school honk around like fools. They peck at each other and are all identical in their plainness and stupidity. I thought a group of geese was called a gaggle, but Charley explained that when geese fly together, it's called a skein. And the chorus girls? They think they're so much better than everyone else, that they fly while the rest of us crawl.

Even from half a gym's length away, I see whispers passing from skein girl to girl like a wave at a baseball game. Mei and Chloe say something to Khadija and they all burst out laughing. Charley walks a little in front of me and heads bravely toward the riser, but I know being laughed at is probably killing her. I may have been ignored in middle school, but Charley was tortured.

We get close enough that I put my backpack down, and the laughter dies away. The only sound now is from the hum of the old lights and Mrs. Miller shuffling music around in her thick binder.

I'm the first one to see it.

Feathers.

All the girls—every single girl on that platform—hold a black feather that they wave in the air with these big smiles stuck on their faces. Even Mei has a feather. Even Chloe.

"What are you doing?" Charley calls out. Her voice isn't loud anymore. I guess it's much harder to rise when it isn't just the three of us.

Yeah, I want to say. *What are you doing?* But no words come out. I look at Mrs. Miller for help. She pulls something out of her binder, snaps it closed, and walks toward the class. "What's with all these feathers?"

The skein girls laugh. They laugh and they laugh and they put the feathers back into bags and pockets and makeup cases and it's like it never happened at all, except that it did.

"Okay, well," Mrs. Miller says. "Attendance, please." And that's that. The three of us sit and stare straight ahead at our teacher. We don't turn around and won't make eye contact with anyone.

Mrs. Miller calls out our names, along with the rest.

Jocelyn Esposito.

"Here."

Charlotte Foster.

"Here."

Brynn McLaughlin.

"Here," I say. "Here. We're here."

Mrs. Miller finishes taking attendance, but it's just like Charley says: the other girls' names don't matter anymore. It's the three of us against the world.

CHARLEY

I hold my binder straight in front of my face and stare at the notes, some connected, some alone, most tied to the staff as if by ribbon or by rope. Up and down, forte or mezzo-forte, sustained or staccato, where we hit the notes and then release quickly, abruptly, an attack.

We're under attack. The feathers, Mei, Chloe, Khadija, Emma, all the skein girls, waving them around, laughing at us.

I haven't told Brynn or Joss, but I've been finding them, the feathers shoved in my locker, in the pages of my math textbook, in my bagged lunch. Yesterday there was a feather in my sandwich. I didn't flinch, didn't react, just threw the whole thing in the garbage like I didn't want it, anyway. I fought through it, got through it. It's what we must endure.

It's what I've always endured.

I got through it in fifth grade, a class trip to the ice-skating rink, where the swirling laughter and the terror and the blades slicing through the cold had been too much for me; I was dizzy and sick and nearly choking, so I'd clung to the side, wouldn't move, couldn't be coaxed away, until the school finally called Mom off her shift to come get me, my classmates laughing, pointing, *what a baby, what a freak*.

I got through it in seventh grade, when Emma had yelled out, *Charley's ACE, Charley's ACE!* I didn't know what that meant, but could tell, just from her tone, that what she was saying was that I was something else. That I was one thing, and that they were another. I looked it up later that night. *ACE. Asexual.* And I remember thinking: probably? Probably I am that. But it hardly seemed to matter. It was just one more difference. One more reason to sit alone when they sat together.

"Brynn," I whisper, now, underneath the music, underneath *Auld Lang Syne*, which we're practicing for our winter concert. "Are you okay?"

"Anxious," she whispers back.

"Mei and Chloe's fault."

"Don't know." But she knows. Shivers. Her ponytail switches like a horse getting rid of flies. The white streak is damp. Plastered to her forehead.

"You're shaking,"

"Window's open. It's freezing."

"Are you sure it's not them?" I turn around and look at Mei and Chloe. Shouldn't, not supposed to, a break in code, but there they are, on the top riser, staring at me. Friends once, fellow empaths. Mei, especially, was very good. She took the rituals more seriously than the others, researched with me, practiced, desperate to help Brynn's mom when she was sick, just like I was.

"Turn around," Mei mouths to me now, moving her index finger in a circle. "Pay attention." She points to Mrs. Miller.

But what I want to know from Mei, what she owes me, what I can't ask out loud, is: If Mei and Chloe told everyone about the Ravens, did they tell the skein the lies about my dad too?

There's no way to ask without stirring those rumors up again, so I listen to Mei and turn back to the piano, even though obeying gives the skein control. For now, anyway. Just for now.

Because my power grows every day.

Late last night, bent over my chime candle, with the milk of the moon spilling through my blinds—I felt a glimpse, a glimmer, of Beyond. Not ghosts, not gods, just energy, just that tingle, like what Ava always talks about. Ava says there's an undercurrent that lives in everything. It's in the grass, the sky, the animals, and if a person is careful, if a person is dialed in, she gets to be a part of it all. Last night, I was dialed in. *This is the year you rise,* the current prophesied. I didn't hear it as much as feel it. A whisper on a moonbeam. And I was elated, glowing, a spark that carried over to this morning, so bright, so happy, that even the sun spoke to me. *Good morning, Charley*, lighting the school on fire.

I take a deep breath. Put my fingers on top of my music. Breathe. Concentrate. The skein's singing swirls around me.

Should old acquaintance be forgot and never brought to mind.

But I push the sounds down, away, so that the singing is an afterthought, nothing but a low hum. I think of my wind chimes' song instead, my new metal columns that dangle from a bronze hummingbird, its jeweled eye glinting, the metal rods colliding in Air, ringing out, *hello, I'm here.*

A sudden gust of wind pushes through the open window. Mrs. Miller's music scatters. The piano stops. Chloe's music comes loose. It flutters to the bottom riser, right near my foot.

"Why is that window open?" Mrs. Miller says. "It's December!"

"I lost my music," Chloe calls out. "Anyone have my page three?"

Brynn looks at me. I look at her. Yes, I nod. Yes, I did that. I'm giddy, elated, nearly laughing, while Brynn bends down and picks up Chloe's music for her, passes it back up the skein, girl by girl, until it gets to the top. Mrs. Miller closes the window, picks up her music, plays again.

The skein continues:

Should auld acquaintance be forgot, and auld lang syne?

Brynn sings. Her voice is pretty and soft. She's the only one of us who actually belongs in chorus. Brynn could even get the winter concert solo if she only believed that she could. She's better than Khadija, even. Better than anyone. And so Brynn sings; the skein sings, but I don't join in. I'm not one of them. I never have been and I never will be. Not that it matters, not that I mind; it's not like I care.

The skein can throw feathers at me. Stick them all over my stuff. Parade them around in chorus, tell everyone about the Ravens. All of that is only for now. Because nobody does that to Dad. Nobody does this to the Ravens. Nobody gets to make Brynn feel *less* when she needs to learn that she is enough, that she is welcome, that she's found a home with me, that the Ravens are home for us all.

• • •

I pop by Dad's classroom during lunch, same as always. The papers are everywhere. There are piles on the desk and on the floor. Dad's wearing his glasses. His book-tie dips onto his desk. He holds ones of his green pens.

"Wild Thursday afternoon?" I ask as I push aside some papers so I can sit on top of his desk.

"Partying like it's 1999 over here," Dad says.

"Which essays are these?"

"The sophomores. *Jane Eyre*."

"Ah. Ms. Bronte. My namesake. How are they?"

"Lazy."

I love hearing about how terrible everyone's essays are. It makes me feel better about myself, which I admit, is lame and predictable, but I'm good at so few things, sometimes I need to prop myself up a little.

"Good."

My dad laughs, that old owl again. He's very handsome in an academic way. My classmates love him even though he's infamous for being crazy about cell phones. If he sees that someone has their phone out, he makes them put it in a bucket in the front of the room. But somehow, he does it in this really cool way that my classmates think is funny. Well, most of them anyway. All of them except for—

"How was your morning?"

"People were mean to me, Joss, and Brynn, in chorus. Same as usual."

"Girls are like that at this age, I'm afraid."

"Not all girls. Not me. Not my friends."

Sometimes I feel so much older than seventeen. That sensation strikes me now as I look around Dad's classroom. He'd hung some work up on the front bulletin board, these character studies of Lady Macbeth, only the better ones up there, one of them, Emma's probably, done in red calligraphy with spots of a deeper scarlet ink around the edges. Supposed to be blood, most likely. *Out damn spot.* But looking at it now, it seems juvenile, silly, the work of a first grader, a second grader. *Look at me,*

Mommy, look at my artwork, Mommy, do you like it? Aren't I smart? I'm embarrassed for her. I wince and then take a deep breath. Separate, separate, she is not me and I am not her. This is my biggest struggle. Brynn's anxiety, Joss's anger, filling me, making me float up, up, a balloon, a feeling of otherness, a feeling of being too far from the ground.

"There are always good people in the world," Dad says. "We have to remember that and search for them and not let go of them once we find them. You're lucky to have such good friends. And such a delightful father."

Things like this, these little signs, these sweet jokes, this is how I know that Mei and Chloe were lying.

"I hope you don't try to make jokes like that during class."

"I don't *try*. I succeed."

"Going back to lunch. Don't party too hard."

"I'll try to keep the volume down."

I head out the door and click it shut behind me.

It's still a good day, after all.

♂OSS

I'm a girl on the run. Couldn't get away from Charley and that school fast enough. Couldn't get into my brother's car soon enough. Now I jump out of the front seat and run toward Malik's rental like I'm a bullet train in a physics problem. I love physics problems.

My brother doesn't wait for me to get into the house safely. Leo revs and peels out like his car is something to show off about. Like his old-ass car wasn't bought from a creepy man on the internet. Like it passed inspection by more than an inch of its life. Everyone's dumb today. Leo and his car. Charley and her feathers. It's not that I don't want to help people. It's not that I don't want to *rise*. I'll fight to the death to help anyone. To help Brynn. Her mom. But feathers? No. I can't believe I have to leave Malik's early to go to the stupid duck pond again.

The rental's metal gate gets stuck as usual and I yank it open. Superhuman strength. I take the concrete stairs two at a time and I'm at the front door, which I rap with my bare knuckles. My pink gloves are tucked away in my pockets. Malik always teases me about these gloves. Says I'm not the kind of girl who wears pink, but I have news for him: I'm not *any* sort of girl. I'm all sorts.

I have to knock hard because there's always music, this bass popping through the floor boards and windows and out onto the street. Malik opens the door and the bass gets louder. It's the noise of a house full of college boys who hide out in their rooms, eating cold Chinese food out of greasy boxes. They're all in desperate need of a babysitter or a mother. But that's not why I'm here.

Malik pulls me into a hug. He's tall and warm and smells like citrus aftershave. That's his signature scent.

"Studying?" I ask.

"How'd you know?"

I touch the frames of his glasses. In the almost six-months that we've been together, I've never seen him wear them before and he looks so academic and adorable that I almost die right there on the front step. Jocelyn Esposito, Cause of Death: Reading Glasses.

"You're late," he says.

"I was with Brynn."

It's not a lie, exactly. It's just that I try to mention Charley as little as possible.

"How's her mom?"

"You gonna let me in?"

"Sorry." Malik laughs and tucks a loose twist behind his ear. He always touches his hair when he's nervous.

He leads me into the kitchen, though to be honest, I'd prefer the living room with the possibility of—the couch. We've only kissed a few times. They were these warm, sweet little pecks on the lips, but that's it. He's Extremely Respectful. Sometimes, I wish he were a little *less* respectful but really, really, really, what a terrible thing to think. Imagine Mom or Dad could hear me? My super liberal, activist parents, with their protest signs spilling out of the closet doors, would have a heart attack hearing me talk like that. Thinking they raised me wrong. They aren't married anymore, but they're still united in one thing: The Pursuit of Justice. And so, I'll *never* speak to them about "less respect" out loud. Can't say it to them and definitely can't say it to Charley, who gets pissed at me whenever I talk about stuff like crushes or kissing.

"Hungry?" Malik sits down at the table where there's a bowl of pretzels and a paper plate filled with sliced apples dipped in peanut butter. "How was your day?"

"How do you think my day was?"

"You know college isn't any better, right?"

Of course, it is. In college, which is now less than two years away, it'll just be me and my aerospace classes and a bunch of people who don't know me. I'll be Jocelyn, Away. It can't get here soon enough.

"Are you gonna be there?"

"Come on. You aren't going to go to county college."

"I know."

"Leo texted that you were with that girl Charley after school again. I thought you—"

"Nah. I was with Brynn. She needed some girl time. Her mom's mammogram and everything."

I want to tell him about the Ravens. I really do. But telling him that would mean I have to tell him about me. I'd have to tell him about the feelings and about the shield I've built up, and I don't think he's ready for that yet.

"What is *girl time* exactly?"

"Huh? It's just like—You've obviously never been a teenage girl."

"Thank God for that."

"Brynn and I aren't so bad, are we?"

Poor Charley. Never gets a shout-out.

"Teenage girls are *the* worst. God help me if I ever have one." Malik grabs at the fruit and cracks it between his teeth. "Apple?"

Cute, but I'm not easily distracted. "Wait. Do you want kids?"

I can picture it. I've seen him with the little boy next door. He gives the boy these giant high-fives every time they see each other. He makes that kid feel important. Brave. Grown. He'd be a good dad. It's actually embarrassing how much thought I've given to this.

He touches his hair. Doesn't answer me. I need a new strategy. "Truth or Dare."

Charley, Brynn, and I play this all the time. *Do you like anyone? If you had to pick only one person at Raine, who would you choose to be your boyfriend or your girlfriend?* I ask Charley this over and over, but she never answers. Someday she'll crack. Wham. Someday she'll tell me.

"Truth or Dare," I say again. "Do you want kids?"

"I didn't say Truth!"

"That's how Brynn and I play it."

"I don't even know what I want for dinner."

"Let's pretend there's a magical mirror. And when you look in the mirror, you get to see your future. Your dream future. What do you see?"

"What do *you* see?" He takes off his deadly glasses and puts them down on the table. Then he looks at me with these big eyes, like he really wants to hear what I have to say. The music's still pumping through the floorboards and I know at least two of his roommates are home. Despite that, it feels like it's just us—alone. And not just alone in the kitchen or the house or his block or New Jersey—we are alone on the earth.

"I'll answer, but don't think for one second that we're not going to come back to you. Okay. I'm working at NASA... far away from here. Somewhere hot. Palm trees. Grandma's memory is back, and she lives with me. I'm really rich, so we get to go on vacation to Sicily every year and Grandma tells us stories about how things used to be."

"Us?"

"Two kids. A husband." I pause. "It's you. Mostly, I see you."

"Hey, so are you some kind of artist or something?"

"Huh?" Feeling like an idiot right about now. "I'm not an artist. I'm a scientist."

"I'm talking about the way you feel. Like when you talk about stuff, you say things I never would have thought of."

"Really? That's how my grandma was. Maybe I inherited it from her."

Before Alzheimer's ruined her mind, Grandma lived in south Jersey, just two blocks from the beach. In the summer, there were dolphins and ice cream and Sunday gravy. It bubbled in a giant pot that Grandma let me stir with a long wooden spoon while she told me stories of the old days in Italy. When she visited, her suitcase sat in the living room for two entire weeks and as long as it was there, I knew adventures were just around the corner. "I couldn't get enough of her. Even when I wasn't with her, I used to hide in the closet in my room and pretend I was talking to her on the phone."

"You hid in the closet?"

Maybe I wasn't tough enough. Maybe I wasn't strong enough. Not big yet, like Leo. Not enough of a *fighter* like Mom was when she brought Leo to the rally about gun laws. Not enough of an *ally* like Dad was, how he supported Mom, even through all their fighting, when she wrote letters to the senators about *my body, my choice*. Maybe I didn't always understand what my parents were upset about, but I knew that the world must be a terrible place. And all of those terrible things my parents and brother knew about the world got all caught in my gut and lived there like a virus.

"Why did you pretend to talk to her instead of really talk to her?"

The signs and the protests and the anger and the news and my parents' loud voices filled me up. The world was so full of hate. The world was so full of ugly.

Grandma, I'd said into my pretend phone. *The meatballs are making my hands sticky.*

"Joss, are you okay?"

I've said way too much. It's making me feel weird, like I'm not strong or something. And if there's one thing I wasn't then, but am now, it's strong. Turn numb in the pursuit of justice. It's the Esposito way. "Somehow, even when we're discussing you, I'm the who ends up doing all the talking. That's enough about me. Tell me what you see in the mirror."

"Oh, I don't know. I never know how to describe things right."

"Try."

He touches his hair.

He's so sad.

It's the sadness that does me in and makes me break Raven code. It's what makes me want to go into the living room. Makes me want to fall onto the couch and kiss him — disrespectfully.

"What do you see in the mirror, Malik?"

He puts both of his hands on his lap and looks down at the table. "Darkness."

"Darkness?"

"Uh-huh."

"But you must see *something*."

"I told you. I don't even see tonight's dinner."

If something's wrong, I'll go to the end of the earth for him if it would help. I'll fight my way through an air raid — anything — for him.

"Should I be worried? Are you…?" I stop. Start again. "Actually, Truth or Dare. Are you…?"

"Shhhhh. Games are for high school kids."

He leans in and puts his lips on mine. I taste peanut butter. He touches *my* hair and time stops. I'm undone.

CHARLEY

It's time.

The salt is coarse and thick and soundless as it tumbles out of the canister. I shake it in a tight circle around our altar and then walk that circle, pacing the trees, while Brynn and Joss wait for me to join them.

We're not great at this yet, but we're better than when we first started, worlds beyond that first time, a year ago now, when Chloe and Brynn had laughed and laughed until the tears fell down their faces, Joss joining them, until Mei and I had to give in and stop. It was a game to them then, no different from playing Light as a Feather at a sleepover or pushing too hard on a Ouija board to get it to spell out words on purpose. But it was never a game to me.

It's definitely not a game here, today, with the air at the duck pond so biting and crisp, later than usual, darker than usual, and with Brynn's mom's scan coming up so soon, with the air that burst through the windows during chorus this morning.

"Northern Guardians, protect our Circle, with your powers of the earth." I try to be still, rooted, to call the feeling of last night's moon back to me. The moon may not hang in the sky yet, but the sun dips very low in the late winter afternoon, backlighting the pond, silhouetting the trees.

Brynn laughs. She always does. I don't know if her laughter ruins it, but I choose to ignore her. Now that Mei and Chloe are banished from our Circle, we will accomplish big, beautiful things together. If I can only focus, really focus, and get Brynn and Joss to join me, the feeling from last night will come back. There's great power in threes. There's great potential here, still untapped. "Eastern Guardians, protect our Circle, with your powers of air."

I push the girls' anxiety away from me and instead, tune into their closed eyes, their hands placed in wait over their knees. "Western Guardians, protect our Circle, with your powers of water."

And then I see it: a shifting of the wind, a ripple over the pond.

Come to me, Water says.

"Southern Guardians, protect our Circle, with your powers of fire."

I sit beside Joss and Brynn and strike a match, which catches and then burns. I cover the tiny flame with my palm and light our candle, which is white, for healing. Despite the wind, it flickers beside Mrs. McLaughlin's flowered scarf.

"Mrs. McLaughlin is perfectly healthy. Her hair is long and thick and there isn't one cancer cell that has re-entered her body."

I hand Brynn a vial filled with pond water. She pours a small drop onto the scarf.

"We cleanse her with this water," I say, and then close my eyes and reach for Brynn's and Joss's hands. Their skin is cold, the sun nearly gone, the moon's turn almost here. "See the power in Mrs. McLaughlin's body. Feel the strength in the muscles of her hand. Feel the universe: The North, the South, the East, the West, fill our space and connect us together. Connect us with her. Connect us with the fabric of the earth. Mrs. McLaughlin, we heal you through the energy of the universe."

"Mommy, we heal you through the energy of the universe," Brynn repeats.

"Mrs. McLaughlin is already heal —" I say, when there's a sudden sound from a nearby tree.

Brynn shrieks and Joss squeezes her hand.

"What was *that?*" Joss asks. "Seriously, what was that?"

"Look!" Brynn points to a branch. A dark bird perches there, his head darting.

A Raven. Our Raven. A sign.

"It's working!"

"A crow," Joss says.

"Not everything's explainable, Joss."

"I'm so freaked out right now," Brynn says.

"Don't be. It's beautiful. It's natural."

It's the first time anything like this has happened during one of our rituals, and I can feel Brynn and Joss's fear entering the Circle. But they shouldn't be scared. It was the universe that brought that Raven to my yard, so many years ago. It was the universe that led me to Dad's office this summer, hunting, looking for evidence about Mei and Chloe's rumors—but finding nothing but that Edgar Allan Poe book, Dad's dog-eared page, *The Raven* poem blinking at me like it was placed there just so I could find it. It's our symbol, a sign, a challenge, our Circle's name.

"Charley, why are we doing this?" Joss asks. Her voice almost derails me—harsh, like the skein, but I recover quickly. This is only Joss, after all. Joss, who feels deeply like I do, and who simply doesn't know what to do with her gift yet. She'll learn.

"Trust that there's a reason."

"What if there's a spirit with us right now?" Brynn asks.

My sweet, shy friend. Brynn doesn't know, doesn't understand, that the sun already speaks to me, that Air listens too, swirling through the skein's music, a joke, a wink. There are spirits everywhere.

"So, what if there is?"

"I wish he would just go away," she nods her head toward our Raven.

"Don't say that."

"Charley," Brynn says. "Are you *only* a good witch, or…?"

"Do no harm, remember? Always." I pick up my feather and gesture for the girls to do the same. We all touch the feathers together. Even Joss.

"Thank you, fellow Ravens. Thank you, Earth, Air, Water, and Fire, for your presence tonight."

"Is she healed now?" Brynn asks.

"Oh, Brynn," Joss says.

"She's healed," I say.

I blow the candle out and grab my friends' hands. We belong to one another, and to the earth. We matter. *I* matter. Brynn's tears fall. We hold hands around the last wisps of smoke.

ʙRYNN

I've never been in trouble at school before. Never. Well, except for that time in second grade when I'd eaten four pieces of Halloween candy after our teacher had said we could only eat two. I look at the paper again. *Plagiarism, See Me.* My God.

I wait for Charley at her locker for ten minutes before deciding she must have already jetted out of school to go to the bookstore. Charley loves Jabberwocky even more than she loves me and Joss. And that's okay. I'm used to it. But I had wanted her to come with me to see Mr. Foster. If there's any kind of perk in having your best friend's dad as your English teacher, this has to be it. Charley would just explain to him I hadn't meant to copy the essay. Not exactly, not really, it's just that *Macbeth* isn't even written in real English.

I'm wrecked. Wrecked, wrecked, wrecked.

"Boo!"

I jump five feet in the air. Maybe six.

"Scaredy cat. What're you still doing here?" Joss asks.

"Where's Charley?"

"Jabberwocky, probably. Why, what's the matter? The skein do something again? Need me to kick someone's ass? Because I *will*. Don't think I —"

I hand Joss the paper.

"Plagiarism? Foster is accusing *you* of plagiarism?"

"I kind of did, though."

I can't breathe. The panic's just in me, the same way the other feelings are inside of Charley and Joss.

"Still, don't worry. Mr. Foster won't get you in trouble."

"Should I tell the truth or lie?"

"Lie."

Joss turns and walks down the hall. Her dark hair fans out behind her. I don't even know why she wants to be a Raven. She's so beautiful and strong. The skein of fools would accept her. No question.

"Hey, aren't you coming?" She turns and comes back to me. As she gets closer, I see that today her nails are sleek and black with sparkles on the ring fingers. I always notice them but pretend not to notice them. Giving compliments is hard. Saying how I feel about anything—including things like Charley's combat boots and Joss's nail polish—is hard.

"Come on. You've got to get it over with." She practically drags me down the hall. We stop when we get to Foster's door.

"Do you have your feather?"

"Why are you asking me that?"

I know Joss hates the feathers. She's just trying to make me feel better. It's really obvious. I'm not dumb like people think. I'm quiet, but I'm not dumb.

"Well, do you?"

Of course, I don't tell Joss I'm onto her, so I touch the front pocket of my backpack.

"It's in here."

I didn't put it in the box Charley gave us yet because I couldn't figure out how to lug that whole thing to school without my parents noticing. Daddy would probably be cool about the Ravens, but Mommy is basically the last remaining loyal Catholic in Raine.

"Then Charley and I are with you, even if we're not with you."

That's not exactly true because I'm a lying liar and my feather doesn't have magical powers, but I can never tell Charley that or she'll disown me just like she did to Mei and Chloe. If that happens, it'll be just like middle school and I won't have any friends at all.

I look through the classroom door. Mr. Foster's sitting at his desk. He leans forward. There are stacks of papers all over the place. I feel like I might faint, like the time when I first saw Mommy with a shaved head. She hadn't looked anything like herself. I'd tried to be brave. I'd tried to say to myself, *this is Mommy, just sick,* but it hadn't worked and *bam.* I'd passed out and cracked my head on the end table of the living room. I had to get eleven stitches and the ER doctor prescribed my pills that very day.

Mr. Foster looks up when I open the door.

Our Father, who art in heaven. The Lord's prayer. I say it and I say it and I say it in my head even though I'm not sure if I believe a word of it anymore.

"Brynn," he says. "Come in."

Why are adults so scary?

This shouldn't be scary. It's just Mr. Foster, who had sent Mommy flowers during chemo along with a giant box of salted caramel cookies for me and Daddy. The nicest teacher in the world, the funniest, the kindest, the one who always makes me feel like… me.

"How you doing? You doing okay?"

He's wearing his book-print tie. Second day in a row. No one wearing a tie like that is scary. That's probably a scientific fact.

"Fine."

"Mom is okay?"

"Fine."

Of course, I don't tell him her scan is coming up. My mouth never lets me say what my brain is thinking. I also don't tell him that right now I'm so nervous that I've got prayers racing through my head on repeat. It's the downside of having gone to Catholic school for elementary and middle, while Joss and Charley went to public school. I have secret lines from Catholic Mass going through my head all day.

I walk all the way over to his desk and place the paper in front of him. I wait about ten or eleven years for him to say something.

"Hey, Brynn? You, okay?"

"Nervous."

"But it's just me, ok? It's just me." He looks at me. And when he looks at me, he *looks*. Sees my eyes. Same as he always does when we have our little chats, our little chats after school, where he tells me to be confident, where he tells me he'll help me grow stronger, to be Brynn, only more, better. Better Brynn. A soft hand on my arm. A tap on my shoulder. *You've got this, Brynn. I believe in you.* It's the same thing Charley says. She says someday I'm going to be lit up from the inside, just like that one weird streak in my hair that everyone asks about. Is it natural? Is that real? *It is,* I mumble. *Born with it.* Charley's working on me. Charley's dad is working on me. I don't mind being a project.

"Just you." I relax. I calm, like he's chamomile tea and I'm drinking him in.

He puts a hand on my hand. It's warm and good, like it always is.

"We have to talk about this, though, even though it won't be pleasant. But it changes nothing about what I think of you. Okay? Nothing changes."

"Okay."

"So, this essay feels different from anything you've written so far."

"It's mine."

"Well, I — Brynn, it's me here. You can be honest with me. I'd like to give you the chance to re-write it, if you just tell me where it came from."

"From my head."

Mr. Foster opens up his desk drawer and pulls out a print-out. Then he turns my paper over and points out a page that he's circled several times with his thick green ink.

"I'm sorry to say this to you, of all people. But it's part of my job, right? Look. Your entire second page matches this online essay word-for-word."

"Maybe I didn't cite it right, but —"

"This isn't about citations."

"No?"

"This is plagiarism."

"No."

"But I'd like to let you re-write it."

He puts his fingers on my waist.

I stiffen. My entire body, stuck. I just stand there. I do nothing. I just stand there.

"I won't tell Ms. Suarez or give you an F. Would you like that?"

His fingers drop lower. Crawl at my thigh.

I'm nearly positive this is happening. I'm nearly positive this is real.

"Yes, I would like that."

I want to die.

We both keep staring down at my paper while his fingers reach around and trace my zipper.

I ignore it and ignore it. Don't move, don't say anything, because who knows what he'll do then?

"Do you think you can finish it this weekend?"

He keeps playing with my zipper.

Suddenly, I'm two people. I'm me, with him, and this is happening, and I'm also me, not here, floating up on the ceiling, watching this happen to someone else from way up above.

"I'll give it to you Monday," I both say and hear myself say.

The me on the ground with him is a statue. Don't move. Don't breathe, even.

"Good."

A final squeeze on my thigh and his fingers go away. His hand returns to his desk and he gives me back my paper, and he's Mr. Foster again. My Mr. Foster. Only not. Only never again.

I grab my essay and fly out of there. I want to run all the way home. I want to burst through walls, leaving Brynn-sized holes in brick. And even while I'm dashing away, I know I shouldn't be running. That I should stand my ground. Tell someone. Why didn't I do anything to stop him? Why did I just stand there? But still, I blow straight past Joss and run to the nearest exit. I can hear her running behind me. I push on the door, but Joss is faster.

Help me, I say to her, but I'm not sure if I actually say it or if I just think it. Everything's blurry. Everything's weird.

What happened? Is he going to tell Principal Suarez? I think Joss asks me this. But I don't really know because I'm still on the ceiling and in my body and Joss is here, but I'm also alone. I've gone crazy, or the world's gone crazy. My brain short circuits. This is what happens when the world explodes.

♪Joss

Brynn explodes out of Foster's classroom and runs to the door. Doesn't stop to say anything to me. He failed her. Didn't think he would. Was actually pretty sure he *wouldn't*. I go after her. She's a blurry mess of jeans and scraggly ponytail. She's a mess all the time. But she's my mess. My Brynnie. Have to watch out for my girl.

"Brynn!" I call out. Faster than her. Faster than anyone. I soar toward the door. Make it just in time to catch her. "What happened? Is he going to tell Principal Suarez?"

She's wobbly. Touches the door frame and leans her head down.

"Is he giving you an F?"

"No," she whispers, so low I can barely hear what she's saying, though I can feel it. I suddenly realize that my armor is lowered. A mistake. Her shame zooms into me, lightning quick. I'm almost knocked over. Suddenly, I know. *I. Know.*

"Is it *the rumors*? Did he touch you?" My shoulders shoot straight up into the air. *Ping*. Warrior mode activated. "I'll kill him. I'll just kill him."

I whip around and head back toward Foster's classroom at a full-on run.

"Joss, wait." Brynn's voice is barely loud enough to hear. "Please, wait. *Charley*."

"She'll understand," I call out, but I stop running.

"It'll destroy her. I don't know what to —" she says, when she freezes like the deer we used to see when Grandma took us to the mountains in Pennsylvania. "Oh God," she whispers. "I feel it."

"Feel it?"

I play dumb because I have to. I play dumb because I'm starting to feel it too and when I feel everybody else's emotions, I get so down and depressed that I can't act on anything. Like I'm a stupid little kid in that closet again, letting my parents and brother do all the work. Feelings aren't worth anything. But action? Action is everything. Action's power. Put that shield back up, girl. Raise that force field.

"His hands. I feel —"

"I'm telling Ms. Suarez."

"Please, Joss. Charley's my best friend."

"So, tell her, then."

Brynn looks at me for a minute, like she's trying to figure me out. She looks at me like I'm an alien from Jupiter.

"You tell Charley first and then we'll come up with a plan for what we're going to do."

"I can't."

"You can. Look, let us drive you home. Leo's waiting for me."

Brynn makes that face. The face she and Charley always make when I say Leo can drive them. He's not that wild a driver. Hurts my feelings.

"I'll walk."

"Fine."

Brynn wants to tell me something. I know what she wants to tell me, too. About the hands. About Mr. Foster. But if I feel that, if I lower my shield again, I'll fall into a well that has no bottom. So, I don't ask her anything. I let her walk out the door. I let her go.

•   •   •

As soon as Brynn's gone, I bust out of school to get away from her as fast as my red sneakers will carry me. If I run fast enough, the anger will burn out. If I get into Leo's car quickly enough, I won't smash Mr. Foster's door open with my fists.

My brother's car is parked on the street just outside of the school's black gate. God forbid he pulls it up the drive so I don't have to run all the way down the road, but Leo and I don't do each other favors. Not our style.

"Jossie! Hey, Jossie!"

Chloe.

I stop dead in my tracks and turn around. Chloe walks toward me with Mei right by her side. The Ex-Ravens. My good friends in middle school. My *not* good friends, now, all because of Charley.

"How are you?" Chloe asks when they finally get close. She's small and blonde and much smarter than the stereotype says she should be.

"My brother's waiting." I gesture toward the car and Chloe giggles and waves. I forgot. She's had a thing for him since my seventh-grade sleepover.

"Hey, so why does Brynn look so upset? We just want to make sure everything's okay," Mei says. "Like with her mom and everything."

Mei's been worried about Brynn since freshmen year, when we found out about the cancer. Mei even pulled an all-nighter once, digging through her mom's old-ass medical textbooks to find out everything she could about metastatic cancer and lymph nodes and different treatment options. *Just in case*, she'd said. *It's irresponsible to ignore science just because we're witches.*

"Everything's good, Mei."

It suddenly hits me. What happened to Brynn in there must be exactly the same thing that happened to them.

"Are you mad at us? We know Charley is, obviously, but…"

"The feather thing wasn't great yesterday."

"I'm sure you understand why we had to do that," Mei says.

"I *kind* of get it," I start to say, "but…"

Juggling, juggling, too many balls in the air.

Here's my issue. I never know how to talk about Charley.

I hang out with her because of what happened during chorus two years ago. Brynn, who none of us knew because she used to go to Catholic school, started crying like crazy, and Charley pulled her off the risers and into the hall. I followed. It's like I was pulled by a magnet. *You feel sad*, Charley said to Brynn. *And now we feel sad*. And while Brynn talked all about how her mom's cancer had metastasized, I was stuck way back there on *and now **we** feel sad*. Charley just knew. She knew even though my shield was raised. *You're an empath too?* I'd asked her. Just admitted it, just like that, because here was someone who could finally, maybe, understand me. Who was a freak just like me and my middle school friends were, but the difference was, she'd given this weirdness a name. I told Chloe and Mei about Charley and the Circle was born and the five of us were stuck like glue ever since.

Until this past summer, of course, when Mei and Chloe had sat Charley down to talk to her about her dad.

"We're just worried about Brynn. That's all," Mei says. "Is her mom okay? We still—like—care about you two. It's just Charley that… I mean. Obviously."

Before I can answer, my phone vibrates, and I take a quick look at the screen.

Charley, the group text starts. *Can we talk?*

Good for Brynn. And even though I know that this is a good thing, the panic hits me so hard I'm almost knocked to the ground. But that's not my fear that I'm feeling. It's Brynn's.

"Look, I gotta go," I say, backing away from them. If they find out what just happened to Brynn, they'll feel *truly* betrayed. Though Charley's the one who banished them, I didn't do anything to help them. Doesn't that make me just as bad as Charley? Am I an accomplice? A bystander? *Me*? Who's meant to fly, save, soar?

Stop, I tell myself. *Don't feel it.*

"Seriously, Joss—hey — are *you* okay?"

"She's not okay," Mei says. "Something's really, really wrong."

"Jossie, you can tell us!" Chloe says. "We've been friends for… how long? We can't let Charley — and all this stupid—witch and feathers stuff get in the way of our being friends. You have to understand why we did that yesterday morning."

Oh, I understand. But if I don't step back from it, I won't be able to fix it, won't be able to get back on the right side of justice. I take a deep breath and raise my shield. Strong, made of iron, nothing gets in and nothing gets out.

"You sure you're okay?"

"I will be—soon."

As long as I run, fly, my red sneakers blazing.

"Jossie?"

But there's no more time. No time to stop. No time to feel. I need to fix this. For Mei and Chloe. For Brynn. I turn on my heels and sprint the rest of the way to Leo's car. Shield up, invincible.

CHARLEY

Brynn's text is the only thing that matters right now.

Charley, can we talk?

Talk about what? About what?

I sense Brynn's fear, sparks flying through the phone, that energy popping and sizzling through space and time and air. I don't know how to harness this feeling, to stop it, to separate my feelings from Brynn's feelings. It all just collides until I'm a nervous wreck, just like Brynn, hands shaking, wanting to sink to the floor.

I want to tell Ava how anxious I am, but even after reading that text, even with the holiday customers smashing into me every three seconds — even then, I can tell that Ava isn't okay enough to listen.

From the outside, she seems perfectly fine. Pretty, even, with her long braids, twisted with silver, that fall below her shoulders. Her pentacle necklace, centered with rose quartz, sits squarely on her neck and looks soft against her dark skin.

Ava sits on the raised platform she had built a little over a year ago, the customers' children squirming as she reads to them from a book of poetry. But inside, in a place that she keeps hidden away, Ava is so devastated that she can barely keep reading to them. I know, because I feel it, too.

I feel everything.

"Oh, hey, Charley," a voice startles me from behind. The invincible tone tells me it's not just one person from school, but a few people. There could be anywhere from three or four of them to a whole half-dozen. *A skein of fools.* That's what Brynn, Joss, and I call them.

"Got your feather in your pocket?"

And I do. Of course, I do.

Yesterday morning in chorus still burns in my stomach. My feathers — our feathers — paraded around like The Ravens are some kind of circus act. The feathers in my locker, my textbooks, my lunch.

"Can I help you with something?" I make my voice flat as I turn around.

As usual, I've said the exact wrong thing. A flash in their eyes and they start fake laughing.

It's so exhausting.

It's so tiring to stand up straight, to be tall, to be brave, while the text makes me nauseous, while the customers smash into me like I'm invisible and while Ava, a few feet away, reads poetry in her full, lilting, actor's voice, when really, deep inside, she's using every atom of energy she has not to crumble into a ball on the stage.

"She needs a book for her brother," one girl says, pointing to their ringleader, who stands in front of them like the first bowling ball pin.

"We know you know all about kids' books."

"Once upon a time, there were four little rabbits…" another girl says.

They erupt into laughter. Kind of real laughing this time, like they can't believe their friend's nerve, but also, they so *can* believe it.

"And their names were Flopsy, Mopsy —"

"Shut up," I say, resorting to this, to stupid words, where if I only wasn't so anxious, I could try to call Air back to me like yesterday in chorus, flip the books from their hands, send them running, afraid, such cowards, out into the night. But instead, my hands shake. Brynn's anxiety or my anxiety, I don't know, but I can't focus, can't think clearly. "Just shut up," I say again.

"Does your boss know you talk to your customers like that?" Their leader nods her head toward silvery Ava, who is still reading to the kids, still shrinking down and down into nothing.

"Charley, Charley, Charley and the Chocolate factory. Better not turn into a blueberry."

"That," I say, quietly, "doesn't even make sense."

"She loves books just like her daddy."

I look over at Ava, whose eyes are now raised. She sees me and she'll rescue me. Even though she doesn't have it in her. Even though all of her fight is gone.

Ava sets the poetry aside and the customers' kids wiggle away, moving toward the rows of books that I had just spent the afternoon stacking. "Ladies," she says, from the stage. "Is there something I can help you with?"

"We're just talking to our friend, Charlotte."

"Charley is very busy, so unless you —"

"That's okay. We're going now."

"Take care of your feather, Charley."

They turn and walk out onto the street, the bells above Jabberwocky jingling, the sound calling me back to a *once upon a time* that was well before the time we live in now. One, two, three, four, five girls, out into the cold, toward the streetlamps of Main Street that are decorated with balls of wired lights and pine.

Raine Hills is a small neighborhood, tucked like a donut hole, inside of a very large New Jersey suburb. Raine is the best of both worlds. It's old school charm nestled in the middle of highways and shopping malls. Hop in your car, zip over to the highway, and suddenly, it's today again, with the rows of department stores and billboard ads. Nothing wrong with that, of course, though I prefer Main Street in Raine to the highway. I'm an old soul. That's what Ava calls me, anyway.

We are two freaks in a pod.

"Hey, Ava, what's the matter?" I ask, as we watch the girls cross the street.

"Shhhh," she says.

And I know, then, that if she talks about it, she will fall onto the ground in grief and never, ever, get up again. The loneliness, especially this time of year, chisels its way into her gut.

I feel it so hard that I gasp.

"Customers," she says. "Children."

"Not now?"

"Not right now."

She puts a hand on my shoulder and it's electric. It's her sadness now in me. I almost topple, but Ava steadies me.

"Stay until closing and I can drive you home?"

I dig into my pocket, brush my hand against the feather, and pull out my phone. The text is still sitting there. I touch the screen, and Brynn's anxiety sparks at my fingertips.

All of this feeling? It's probably magic.

I close Brynn's text and write a message to Dad. Dad, who I have to protect now, again, this time from Mei and Chloe spreading those lies about him not just through our small Circle, but all around school, just like they did with the feathers, The Ravens.

Staying late. Ava will drive me home.

"Good," Ava says from over my shoulder.

Yes, it *is* good. Ava, shrinking, Ava, sad, will drive me home.

Our quiet times in the car together are moments I hold in the palm of my hand, clasping Ava's wisdom for later, when I need to feel calm, settled, when the feelings get too big to hold. She'll drive me home. She'll set me straight.

I go back to the books, which, of course, now need to be re-stacked. A few customers file out, and a few file in, the bell signaling and re-signaling an older, better world. The world of Dickens' London. The world of Hemingway's Paris. The balls of light from the street make pictures on our darkening windows. The night is quiet. The magic goes still.

• • •

All the house lights are on. The entire bottom floor is lit, as well as the bedrooms upstairs. Mom never sleeps, so the den light is to be expected, but the other rooms are a surprise.

"Does this mean your dad's still awake? Isn't it late for him?" Ava turns the heat up in the car as we sit in the driveway and sticks her fingers right up to the vent.

"Grading papers, I guess? I don't know."

"Have you heard anything more about —"

"Rumors. That's all."

I wish I had never told Ava about this. But I had to tell someone, didn't I? There had to be somewhere for that hurt to go, some kind of release.

"I want to say something to you," Ava continues, "but I don't want you to get angry or take it the wrong way or think that I'm not on your side. Because I'm always on your side. You know that, right?"

Ava is my compass, my North Star.

"I believe them," Ava continues. And she says it like she is ancient, like she once lived in the Egyptian pyramids, or drew symbols on cave walls. "I believe those two girls. And I think maybe you should encourage them to speak up."

"It's just gossip. You've seen how they treat me. Even tonight at the store, you could see it."

"Were Mei and Chloe part of the group of girls who came in tonight?"

They weren't, though I don't say so. I feel like it's a leading question. But Ava interprets my silence.

"Then you can't lump them into the same category as the others. People aren't as easily compartmentalized as you'd like to think."

"Mei and Chloe are just trying to get me to crack, same as the girls tonight. It's all anyone's been trying to do since, like, first-grade."

"One time... I..." Ava drifts off, doesn't finish her thought. The sadness engulfs her. And because of that, it engulfs me. "I think those girls were very brave to tell you. They trust you."

"They just need me for something."

"Is it so terrible to be needed? Isn't that why you created your Circle in the first place?"

Ava is the only adult who knows about the Ravens. She knows about the magic. She has never once doubted me, never once laughed. She's the one who first gave me some chime candles and oils, and suggested I blog about my spells. She knows I formed our Circle so that Joss, Brynn, Mei, Chloe, and I could use our empathy to help people. But even with all of that knowledge, I can't listen to her about Dad.

"Mei and Chloe are liars," I say to Ava.

She purses her lips, shakes her head at me. Then she takes her fingers away from the vent and, foot on the brake, moves her gear into reverse, the end of my driveway appearing in her backup camera. It's my signal to get moving. She doesn't want to talk about why she's so sad, why I can feel it coming off of her in waves, why I'm breathing in her pain.

I grab my backpack, open and close the car door.

"Love you," she mouths.

"Love you back," I say, out loud, into the chill, my breath coloring the air.

I hear Ava's car back out of the drive and head down our street. I don't turn back to wave.

♂JOSS

We drive with the windows down. It's not just air coming through them. It's wind.

"We're going to die of hypothermia," I yell over the roar.

It's late on Friday night and we're speeding through suburbia with its hipster moms and dads and sleepy toddlers being pulled in and out of car seats and lugged into boring chain restaurants. But not us. We'll drive straight through the suburbs until we pop out in Warden, which is where Sebastian's Restaurant and Malik's rental house sit, waiting for us.

"It's not *that* cold," Leo yells back.

"Being extra."

Leo laughs and pumps the gas. He swerves around a sloth-level slow driver and zips through the light just before it switches to red.

But even with the freezing air and incredible speed and even as we get further and further away from Raine, I can't get this afternoon out of my head.

I kick my feet at the glove compartment and the door swings open.

"Watch it," Leo says.

This car is old as hell, but it's ours. I reach down to close the door. There's a map in there. An actual map.

"How old is this car, exactly?" I ask.

"Old enough to know better."

Old enough to know better was Grandma's favorite thing to say to us before Alzheimer's ruined her mind.

"Snake Guy kept maps?"

"You expected Snake Guy to be more high tech?"

We'd bought the car from some weird guy in Warden who kept tanks of snakes in his living room. I thought we were going to be serial-killed in broad daylight and kept giving Leo *let's get out of here* looks, but my brother really wanted the car. He'd worked over-time to buy it, serving wings and beer that he wasn't even legally allowed to drink yet.

"You hungry?" Leo asks.

"Starved."

Leo swerves to make a quick turn, and this time, our car screeches through the intersection just *after* the light turns red. There's an angry horn, but we're so used to it that the sound barely registers.

We fly past the malls and parking lots and soon the older houses show up outside our windows. The fences around these houses switch from iron to wood and back again, trying to protect homes that have started leaning into the ground. Some of them are abandoned. Some of them hold families who work and work for all that they have — which isn't much, but just like our car — it's *theirs*. Warden is everything Leo wants to achieve. Who cares if he'd be leaving our house? Who cares if he'd be leaving stuffy, old-school Raine and Dad with his rules? Warden is possibility. It's independence. It's escape.

"Next year," Leo says.

He says this every single time we drive around Warden.

"You buyin' dinner?" I ask.

"As if you have any money."

"I have money. I choose not to spend it."

"Spoiled."

Leo swerves around another slow driver. I throw my feet up onto the dash. Try to ignore everything but the speed and the wind. The cold is a drug. The cold is a high.

We're invincible.

•   •   •

It isn't much to look at, but Sebastian's has always been our spot. It was our place even before Leo started working here. There's a fake fireplace against the wall, right next to a stack of unused chairs. I don't know what they're waiting for with these extra chairs. They should have dumped them years ago but are probably holding out hope that someone will book Sebastian's for a retirement party or something. Dad always says: *Sebastian's is charming, but I wish you two wouldn't spend so much time there.* Dad calls everything that's run-down "charming" or "adorable" When it comes to me and Leo, Dad turns into a ferocious beast. It's like we're these little precious cubs he wants to keep tucked away in a cave while he goes out and battles bears in the woods. Doesn't work like that, Dad. Maybe they didn't mean to, but he and mom raised two kids who would go fight right beside him. Who are ready to run. Spread out. Fly. Wait till he sees the *charming* place Leo plans to move into next year.

My brother and I slide into our usual booth. Some guy I don't know and Malik are both on shift. Malik and I will have to do our dance routine. It's this weird choreography we've come up with where we know we're happy to see each other but can't show it too much or Leo will start acting weird. Malik brings our sodas before he even brings the menus. Leo says it's really easy to avoid ringing soft drinks up and that they're pretty cheap to make, so I never feel bad about taking the free drinks.

"What's up?" Malik leans over our table. His hair is tied back in a ponytail, so I can see there's a pencil behind his ear. As if he needs it. As if there's not only one other table of middle schoolers in the restaurant. I can't believe they're only a few years younger than me. They look like infants. Their server, the guy I don't know, leans over their table, trying to look all suave. Why? They're like twelve-years-old.

"Picked her up at school earlier. Her friend wouldn't get in the car. Scared of me, probably."

"Don't flatter yourself. Which friend?" Malik asks.

"Brynn," I say quickly.

"Yeah, Brynn. Though that Librarian Girl never drives with us, either," Leo says.

"Librarian?" I ask.

"The book-girl."

"Charley?"

"You're going to get your ass kicked, hanging out with her." Leo says.

"Oh yeah? By whom?"

"By *whom?* Are you her Librarian-in-Training?"

I give Leo my famous ice-queen stare. Malik isn't expecting it. Doesn't really know that I'm a completely different person around my brother. He laughs and takes a small step back. The pencil falls off of his ear and he bends down to pick it up. I study him out of the corner of my eye. He's so handsome.

"What are you guys eating?"

"Burgers," I say. "And I want to see blood dripping on the plate."

"How 'bout I just bring you a live cow?"

"Do you have one back there? No wonder you got so many health code violations last year."

"Shhhh," Malik says, as a few new customers swing the door open. It makes the cold rush in. "You can't say that out loud." He puts a finger up to my lips. I wish his lips were on my lips instead, but I'll take what I can get. Even his finger is kinetic. Yep — Physics is still my favorite class.

"Can you bring it out fast? I'm meeting my mom after," my brother says.

The new customers look around like they're expecting a hostess to seat them. Malik exaggeratedly gestures for them to sit wherever they want.

"Raine people," he says quietly, just to Leo and me.

"Um. You used to be a Raine person. *We're* Raine people."

"You're different." Malik winks at me and then goes to take care of his new table. He doesn't take his pencil off of his ear. I was right. It's just a prop. When he finishes with them, he strolls into the kitchen. He looks like he doesn't have a care in the world, but I know better.

Leo told me that Malik used to live in Raine, not too far from our house. When he was in sixth grade, his mom died, leaving Malik and his dad by themselves to figure things out. As soon as he turned eighteen, *boom*, Malik got a job and took out a bunch of college loans so he could live on his own, leaving his dad in Raine in this big, old, empty house. But even if Leo hadn't told me any of that, I'd still know that Malik is the saddest person I've ever met.

"Hello?" Leo snaps at me. "Did you want to just eat dinner with Malik, or what?"

"Sorry."

"Whatever, moving on. So, does Librarian Girl still carry a feather around with her all the time?"

"Doubt it." I sip my soda. The machine doesn't have enough syrup in it. Tastes like seltzer with brown food dye thrown in. "And anyway, even if she did, I don't like it when you make fun of her. At least Charley and Brynn are real. I hate fake people."

"If you were turning into a freak like them, you'd tell me, right? Like if their freak juice was oozing into you, too, you'd let me know? Or would you not even realize it? Maybe it's more like being bitten by a vampire."

"Freak juice?"

"You know what I'm saying, right? Like if Librarian Girl is the head of a cult or something. There's a vibe. You can't deny it. Just because Brynn follows her around like a sad puppy doesn't mean—"

"Please, shut up. You don't know what you're talking about. Brynn's mom was really sick a couple of years ago."

Saying Brynn's name out loud reminds me of this afternoon. I take out my phone. No texts from Charley. Weird.

"You instagramming our sodas? Because seriously, no one cares."

"Are you even still on Instagram?" I ask, keeping my brother distracted while I open up my browser and hit refresh on Charley's blog. I've refreshed the site at least six-hundred times since I left school. There's nothing there but the same old entry: *Tried using crushed violet tonight. The aroma awakened the stars.* What is that? What does that even mean? But I'm not on the site just to torture myself. If Brynn talked to Charley about what happened, Charley will head straight to her blog to write about it in some kind of book quote code no one will understand except for her. That's what she did when Mei and Chloe talked to her over the summer.

"If the food ever comes, we gotta eat fast. You can't like take pictures of it or whatever and pray your boyfriend takes pity on you and gives it a little heart."

"What are you and mom doing, anyway? It's so late."

"Don't know yet." Leo pauses. "But hey, you want to come?"

He's an asshole, but he's my brother, and he loves me. He knows I get crazy-jealous that he gets along with Mom better than I do.

"Homework."

"Homework? On Friday? Librarian-girl really *is* rubbing off on you."

"We're nothing alike. I'm going to be a scientist. She's a writer."

"She's a witch."

I stop refreshing the blog and throw my phone back into my bag when there's a shriek from the table next to ours. Both of the middle schoolers are laughing, but one of them is bright red and touching her back.

"Um, that really hurts, you know," the girl's friend says to the server, who's cracking up. Or pretending he's cracking up, anyway.

"Wouldn't know. Don't wear one of those." He touches his chest, smiles at them, and goes back into the kitchen.

The girl's embarrassment comes out of her in waves. It's the same shame I'd felt this afternoon when Brynn had busted out of Mr. Foster's room like that. Feels a little hard to breathe. But no. That's Brynn's anxiety. That's this middle schooler's humiliation. Shut it down. Shut. It. Down.

"Who's that idiot?" I say to my brother.

"Who, Caleb? He's harmless."

"Not harmless to her."

"How do you know?"

"Don't be that guy." I blow right past my brother's question. It's not even worth trying to explain the feelings or the shield to him. Because, unlike Charley, I know that all of this feeling isn't magic. It's just pain. It's just fear.

"Don't be *what* guy?"

"Just be better. Be Dad."

The kitchen doors open again. If anyone can make me feel better, it's Malik. I turn, ready to give him my best smile, but it's not him. It's that guy Caleb again. He's completely covered in grease and carries out our plates, which he throws down in front us. The fries are piled high and covered in salt. At least Malik plated them for us. I can tell.

"You're lucky you're skinny," Caleb says to me.

My already clenched teeth lock down harder.

"She doesn't talk?"

I close my eyes. Shield: Activated. Let him think I'm a complete freak; I don't care. If I don't shut him out, I might start throwing things.

"Can you tell Malik I wanted a milkshake, too?" Leo says to him. Completely oblivious as usual.

"What about you?" Caleb says to me.

I don't answer.

"Hello? What's your problem?"

Ignore.

"What, not even a smile?"

"Forget my sister. She's being weird."

Caleb scribbles something down and then he leaves our table. He crosses back over the floor and pushes into the kitchen, which is good for him, because if he didn't leave us alone, I was going to punch him in the face.

"Joss, the hell are you doing?" Leo asks. "Be nice to him! I work here. You want me to keep driving you around places, I need gas to do it. And this job puts gas in the car. You need me to have this job. You need *me*."

The things my brother doesn't know about me could fill books. I don't need anyone. I don't need anything. I keep my eyes closed and block it all out. My rage cools in the darkness.

ᗷRYNN

When I'm alone in my room, away from Mommy and Daddy, the hands come back.

I pull the blankets up to my chin so I can hide from the furniture and from the TV and from my lavender curtains, but I can't settle down. Willow burrows into the nook at my hip.

"Should I call Charley, kitty?" I ask. "Do you think that's a good idea?"

But Willow doesn't have any answers.

I never call people, but Charley didn't answer my text and this might be an exception, like a kind of emergency. I pick up my phone. Look at it. Willow gets up and rubs his chin on the screen.

"Stop, kitty," I say. "Naughty Willow." I scratch his ear.

I can't call Charley. Too hard.

Just close your eyes, Brynn. Just try to sleep.

But let's be honest. I'll never sleep again. Every time I drift off, I see Mr. Foster's hands and jolt awake.

If I could just call her! It shouldn't be this hard. Charley always says she's here for me, doesn't she? She always says I matter, that I need to learn that I'm important. And isn't this important?

Okay. Oh God, okay.

I call.

Willow looks at me like he has a question, but since I don't know the question, I definitely don't know the answer.

The phone rings.

It rings and rings. Goes to her voicemail and I hang right up. Why is she ignoring me? It was just a text. *Charley, can we talk?* How could she know anything from that?

The panic is in me. It's full-on now. It's probably eleven out of ten or fifteen out of ten. Singing won't help. The feather definitely won't help.

"Willow?" I call him closer. Rub his chin, touch the little gray dot on the bottom of his white neck. "What did I do to deserve this?"

Well, the rituals, right?

I pull the covers to just below my nose and Willow gets impatient with me. He jumps off the mattress and darts under the bed. He'll stay there until morning. I wish he would come back.

Kitty, I think, trying to send him a message underneath the bed. *Do you think I should take a yellow pill?*

I could take a few. Enough to drift away, to get rid of the hands, to forget about Charley not answering me, and to sleep peacefully through the night.

No. That's a bad idea. That's a terrible bad idea.

I erase the pills from my mind.

What else? What can I do to calm myself down? I could maybe call Mommy and Daddy up here, but even if I do, I can't tell them about Mr. Foster. One word about it and they'll be at the police station or at the school with their swords raised in the air. And then: Charley lost. Charley broken. Because of me.

I feel so — small. So trapped.

Stop staring, I say to the walls, but the sound is muffled beneath my blankets. *Don't look at me.* I close my eyes but I still see the hands.

I call Charley again.

The hands come back, and the hands come back.

CHARLEY

The moon has always talked to me.

On a July night, when I was about six-years-old, my parents were sitting out on our deck after dinner while I roamed the yard below. Though I'd pretended not to be paying attention, I could hear them up there, their voices tight and angry.

I found a giant stick that I could use as a smasher to whack the tree trunks. I thwacked a tree just as a lightning bug came near. I dropped the stick and cupped my hands.

Follow it, said the moon. *Catch it.*

You could be arrested! Mom's voice carried out to me. It was so cold and so serious. I didn't know what my parents were talking about, but I knew from their tones that it was very grown-up.

I followed the lightning bug, which landed on a tall blade of dry grass, just as the porch door slammed and Mom was gone.

And that's when I saw it. A bird, its feathers black and sleek, laying on its side in the grass, its beaded eye wide open. I'd never seen anything lie so still.

Daddy! I had screamed.

He ran down from the deck and joined me on the grass, his grown-up drink hanging from one hand. His feet were bare, his toes touching the dry earth. The lightning bug was gone, but the pale moon lit his way toward me.

Oh, Daddy had said. *Oh, the poor thing.* He put a hand on my shoulder.

Help her, Daddy.

I can't help her, Charley, I'm so sorry. She's not in her body anymore.

Where'd she go?

The moon's got her. The sky's got her. She's free now. Do you understand?

I didn't understand.

Daddy, is the moon bad?

Of course, not. The moon's what tells us we're not alone.

I grabbed his hand. The firefly circled again. The little bug was trying so hard to light up the dark. I held Daddy's hand tightly, tightly, so that the moon wouldn't take him, too.

• • •

I take a deep breath, steady, Charley, steady, take off my coat, fling it over my desk chair, take the feather out of my pocket and slip it into its silver engraved box, along with the candles and oils and my beaten-up copy of *iWitchcraft: Rituals in the*

Digital Age. Calmer, better, just me, the moon, my walls' black paint, the hurricane offshore, raging yes, but outside, far away.

But then Mom's at my door. She knocks once and opens it, looks at me, up and down, thinks I don't notice this, but I do, the way she hates my new boots.

"I didn't hear you come in," she says.

Mom wasn't on shift at NICU this afternoon, so she doesn't smell like babies, which is too bad, because she always seems slightly gentler when she has that baby smell on her. Despite not being on shift, she's tired. Her internal clock is not aligned with Dad's and mine.

"How was work?"

"Crazy. Holiday shopping."

"Thanksgiving's barely over!"

"Retail doesn't work like that, Mom."

"I forget that you're an expert businesswoman now."

She doesn't mean to be so snippy. Dad has been telling me this for as long as I can remember. *That's just how she talks,* he used to say, when I would run to him, crying about the way Mom had said I didn't need a Band-Aid, or that I would have to 'just get over it' when I'd left my stuffed bear at Grandma's. It was Dad who drove me all the way back to Grandma's house, one hour, both ways, to get Bear back. It was Dad who understood that Bear was family.

"Ava's teaching me," I say. "Dad's asleep?"

"Fell asleep in the den, I guess. I haven't seen him."

My phone vibrates again, and I pull it out of my pocket. Brynn calling me instead of texting. I don't think she's ever called me before, not in the two years since we've been friends.

I don't want to answer it. It's not fair, I shouldn't have to, not here, with the black paint and the books and the glowing, iridescent stars. I look at Mom, ask her without asking her, *what should I do?*

"Is someone calling you?"

"Uh-huh."

"A friend?"

Like I couldn't have a friend? Like maybe Charlotte Grace Foster, super freak, couldn't possibly get a phone call on a Friday night?

"Brynn."

"Is her mom okay?"

The phone stops, goes still.

"Mom? I feel... really weird."

"What's going on? What does she want? Just say it."

Mom's tone, so quick, so fast, so assuming. Never mind.

"I don't know what it's about. I won't know until I answer, right?"

Mom rolls her eyes deep into her head. "I was just—asking, right? Just—checking in."

"Sorry. I'm sorry."

She sighs, shuts my door. I'm rude to her. She's quick-tempered with me; there's this anger between us, floating, like dust in light. I don't know how to make it go away.

My phone vibrates again, lights up, glowing, slightly green.

I don't want to answer.

But with magic comes responsibility. It's rule number two of the Raven Code, falling right behind our most important tenet: do no harm. And I'm a good witch, a doer of white magic, magic that has grown and deepened and expanded, so that it's my duty to use it, to harness it, to direct it toward the light. And Brynn? Brynn's one of my best friends. Brynn, Joss, and Charley: our names wound together, like a braid. And my friend is sad tonight. She needs me. I can feel it; I know.

I take a deep breath, slide my finger over the screen to accept the call.

"Hey, Brynn." There's a sound on the other end, like something's caught in her throat. "I'm here. Are you okay?"

But she doesn't have to speak for me to know that she's in pain, that she's been gutted. I feel all of that as I keep the phone close to my ear and climb into bed, still with the purple bulb lit, still with clothes on.

"Brynn. Seriously, what's the matter?"

Nothing. Silence.

"Hey, I love you, okay?"

I don't know what's wrong, but it's something dark, something terrible, something large, that tries to get into my room, tries to get through the window, to dig into my sacred spot, my room, with the black paint, the glow-in-the-dark stars.

"I'll stay on the phone with you tonight," I say, after a while of silence. "And then I'll come see you in the morning. Joss, too. We've got you. We've both got you, you know that. I love you. Okay? No matter what happened, I love you."

She says nothing, but she hears me. Relaxes a little, breathes more slowly. My best friend, my sweet Brynn, who doesn't know that she's worth so much, that she's worth millions, diamonds, gold, glistening, that wild white streak a clue, a sign, an indication. I want to teach her this one thing. I want her to know.

"Good night, bestie," I say.

I put my head down on my pillow and toss the blankets off, keeping the phone beside me. The hurricane beckons. The hurricane's close. But not here, please, not now. I close my eyes. Keep them shut. Brynn's still on the other line as I drift off to sleep.

Brynn

"Why do you have so much construction paper?" Joss asks. "Who has this much paper?"

"It's been here since I was little. I don't know."

"We could make a sick collage."

Joss fans through the paper and then throws it on the desk. Her nails are still that slick, glossy black.

"I don't know what we're going to say to Charley." I stare at Joss's nails but still don't tell her I like them. "I'm so-"

"Anxious. I know." She takes out a pair of scissors and pulls a red piece of construction paper from the stack. "Can I cut this up?"

I want to say something. Need to say something but I'm not sure if I'm thinking clearly. I'd barely slept all night. "I think," I say really slowly, "that maybe you don't realize how much this is going to upset her."

"Oh, I realize. I just don't care."

"It's our job to care."

"Yeah, but turn that around on yourself. It's our job to care about you, too."

"I'm not as important."

"Not as important as what?"

"Charley."

"Do you really think that's true?" Joss puts my scissors down next to the leaning stack of paper and scoots next to me on the rug. "You can tell me."

"The world needs her."

"That's a little dramatic." Then she softens her voice. Looks at me like she can see through me. "How are you feeling?"

"I'm so scared that Charley —"

"I don't mean about Charley. I mean—about what happened yesterday."

"I'm fine."

"You're such a liar."

"I think it will be a mistake to tell her. Look what happened to Mei and Chloe! She kicked them out. For this. For this same thing."

"She won't do that to you. You're her best friend."

"How do you know she won't?"

"Look. I —I don't know. I don't know, really. But if she does kick you out, then *she's* the one who's wrong, not you."

"If you think she might kick me out, then we can't tell her!"

"Listen, don't you remember what Charley said? This is the year we rise."

"Of course, I remember."

"Then she'll understand that this is how we're going to help. This is the Ravens' contribution."

The doorbell rings.

I hear Mommy's feet pad over to the door and can picture her pulling it open and wrapping Charley up in one of her famous hugs. Their voices carry up to us. Laughing and light.

"The moon's still out!" we hear Charley say to Mommy. "Did you see it? It's very beautiful."

"I haven't been out yet this morning. Not an early bird like you ladies. Jocelyn is upstairs already."

Joss and I sit very still as we listen to Charley's feet hit the bottom of the staircase.

"Mrs. McLaughlin," Charley calls out from the stairs. "We're all thinking about you."

"Thank you, sweetie," Mommy says. There's a little sadness in her voice. A little caution.

The room swells when Charley enters it. Not literally, obviously, but that's always what it feels like to me. It's like there's a shifting of the light or a movement in my purple curtains. I'm pulled toward her like we're opposite poles of a magnet.

She comes in and shuts the door really fast so Willow can't get in. Charley doesn't like cats. They make her sneeze. I always think that's funny. A witch who hates cats.

Charley takes off her thick puffer coat and puts down her very full-looking backpack. Her sweater doesn't match her tights, but somehow it looks right. Her red hair isn't brushed. It juts out at weird angles, filled with static from her winter hat. Her freckles are little compasses that point from her forehead to her chin. Her skin is so white that it seems to glow in the dark.

"Are you okay?" Charley asks me. She doesn't say hi or anything. "I've been really worried."

"She's not even a little okay," Joss answers for me.

I shake my head at Joss, as if I can get her to be quiet when everyone can see—the desk, the rug, even—that I have no voice here.

"I brought the stuff. We can do an extra spell for your mom for Friday." Charley paces around the room like a tiger in a cage.

"Charley?" Joss says. "Sit down, please. We want to tell you about something that happened yesterday."

"Do you have the headscarf, Brynn? If not, it's not that big a deal. We can still —"

"Brynn had to see your dad after school."

"No," Charley says.

N-o. Just two letters. A plain and simple word, but it almost kills me.

"Yeah, she did. Listen. I walked her over to his classroom because she was completely freaking out," Joss says.

"Was she having a panic attack?" Charley stands near my desk with one hand on the construction paper.

"No," I say. Those same two letters.

"Yes," Joss interrupts. "So anyway, she went in there while I waited for her in the hallway. A few minutes later she came out, running toward the exit, in full-on panic mode."

"I wasn't in full-on —"

"Well, I heard him ask to see her because of her essay, so. I guess so."

"Yes, exactly," Joss says. "Because of the essay. Charley, sit down. Please."

Charley looks Joss dead in the eye—and then sits. Joss crawls closer to her. "Listen. Listen for a minute. Now that it's Brynn, and not just one of those skein girls, we know that it's actually true and we can do something about it."

"Do something about what?"

"You know what," Joss says, really quietly. "You know what. And it's our responsibility to do something about it."

"You said she was panicking before she even went in there. Why shouldn't she be panicking when she came out? What's wrong with you guys? Why are you doing this to me?"

"We're not doing anything to you. We love you."

"How could you?" Charley asks. "Did you see it happen?"

"No, but —"

"Then how do you know?"

They both look at me. Both of them. And they both need the complete opposite thing from me at the same time.

"What do you mean?" Joss's gone straight to yelling. "I know because Brynn *told* me. Just like Chloe and Mei told *you*."

"She's lying," Charley says.

"She isn't! Can't you feel that? Don't you just know that it's true? Look at her for a second."

"She always looks like that."

"Charley!" I say. And I can't help it. The tears fall down my face. I wipe at them, but it doesn't help. There are friends in my room right now. Right now! For the first fourteen years of my life, the only people who ever set foot in my bedroom were Mommy and Daddy and my cousins. No one from school ever came over and no one ever invited me.

"You do. You always look like this. You always feel like this. Even on just a normal day, I feel your anxiety at the same level as it is right now."

The darkness in Charley's voice is going to wreck me more than Mr. Foster's hands did. I think of Mei and Chloe and how one minute they were with us at the duck pond and the next minute, they weren't. The next minute, they'd organized the skein into torturing us with those feathers. How fast friends go away. How fast friends are thrown out like trash.

"You're right," I say quickly.

"Brynn," Joss says.

"I made it up. I made the whole thing up."

"*What?* What are you doing?" Joss says.

"How could you do that to me?" Charley's eyes are wide and angry.

"I didn't want to fail the essay."

"No," Joss says. "Brynn, that's enough. Charley, you're the one who told us that this is the year we rise. And here's our chance. The Ravens' very first chance to help people who really need it. Who knows how many girls this has happened to at school? If it happened to Mei and Chloe *and* Brynn, there have to be more. There have to be many other people who are hurting that we can help."

"Please, please forgive me," I say to Charley, completely ignoring Joss.

"I don't know why you would—you're my best friend."

"Yes, yes, I'm your best friend. I still am. I just— I'm so stupid, Charley. You know how stupid I am."

"You're not stupid! Stop saying that!" Joss says.

"And I thought he would tell Principal Suarez that I had plagiarized and I had never been in trouble before and I remembered what Mei and Chloe had said, so I told Joss it happened to me too—like I can't believe I did it. I'm so sorry."

"That's like messing with someone's *life* over an essay. My dad's life. My life. You can't do that!"

"Please forgive me. Please don't kick me out."

"Brynn! Stop it!" Joss says.

I can't stop crying. Charley stares at me for a long time.

"*Please*, Charley."

"I know you have a ton of stuff going on with your mom," Charley finally says.

"I do, yeah. I really do."

"You haven't been thinking clearly. If you were having a panic attack, then you weren't thinking straight."

"I-I wasn't. Not that that's a good excuse, but —"

"That's why you did it, right? Because you were panicking? That's why, right?"

"Yes, of course, that's why. Of course."

"You can't ever, *ever* pull something like that again."

"Of course, I won't. Never. I promise."

"Then I — I forgive you."

"Oh, God, thank you."

"It's what friends do, right?" she asks.

"Right. Right!"

But then out of nowhere, out of thin air: the panic rises up again. If Charley's going to forgive me, why don't I feel better?

"Hey, are you okay?" Charley asks me.

"You're not listening to her," Joss says. "She's trying to tell you something really, really important and you're ignoring her. Just like you ignored Mei and Chloe. Just like we *all* did."

Their voices are swimming and far away and I probably need a yellow pill. I suddenly can't speak.

Can barely think. It's like an invisible globe glows around me, and Joss and Charley are stuck outside of it while I'm inside. They don't see the globe. They don't know that I'm alone while they're together.

"Is it your mom?" Charley leans close. "Is it her mammogram?"

"Friday," I whisper. Charley is so near to me I almost reach out and touch her, but the globe makes that impossible.

"Okay. Well, okay," Charley says. "The Ravens, back in action. Does everyone have their feathers?"

"*Charley*," Joss says.

"It's… mine's in here."

I get up, go into my closet, and pull my feather out of the box that Charley gave us. My body freezes up. If I were really a witch, wouldn't I have some crystals and candles at my house, too?

"I don't really have much stuff."

"I told you, I brought some things."

"Oh, oh, okay. But please, not the salt. Mommy will —"

"Just the crystals and candles. Okay?"

It's not really a hundred percent okay, because I worry Mommy will smell smoke, but I agree anyway and get up to lock the door before settling back on the floor with Charley and Joss.

"We don't need to go full-out like usual. Just send your intention out into the universe. That's what Ava does." Charley holds her feather out in front of her and I do the same. Charley and I layer our feathers, one on top of the other, while Joss just stares at us.

"The Ravens," Charley begins.

"The Empaths," I say.

We look at Joss. She doesn't say anything.

"The Girls Who Feel Too Much," Charley fills in for her. She acts like it doesn't bother her that Joss isn't participating. But how couldn't it? I try to make eye contact with Charley, but she's staring down at the feathers. She hands me a crystal and tells me to keep it in my palm.

"Now, hold this in your mind. Mrs. McLaughlin is healthy and strong. Picture her strength. See how solid she is. Send that out to the universe."

Charley covers my hand with hers, and we hold the quartz together.

"Mommy is healthy and str —" I start to say, when there's a sudden sliding sound and then a loud crash.

"What was *that*?"

My eyes flash open. The entire stack of construction paper fell off my desk. Most of it is now in a messy pile, but a few pieces of blue and violet separated from the rest and slid across the rug.

"Wow," Charley says.

"Come on," Joss says. "I was playing with that before. This is ridiculous. Like I can't believe either of you right now."

"Shhhhh. There's magic here," Charley says. "This is the second time now that I —"

"I feel it!" I can't help myself. I want to be back on Charley's team, where it's glittering and bright, where she isn't mad at me anymore. "I really feel it!"

"It happens every time we touch," Charley says.

"It just — it feels like you're not alone." Joss gives me this look, like she's trying to see into my soul. "That's all it is."

"The moon tells us we're not alone," Charley whispers. "My dad said that to me once after I'd found a dead bird. A raven."

Charley's dad. Mr. Foster. The hands. But no. Don't think about that now. That doesn't matter.

"You found a raven?" I ask instead.

"And I always knew that it meant something, that it was a message."

"A message?" I whisper. "For us?"

"A message that there's something here beyond what we can see. There's a reason we were brought together. I've always known it."

"You're being so mean to her," Joss says to Charley. "You're being a terrible person. I can't even look at you right now."

Joss doesn't know what she's talking about. Charley's back to herself again. She feels the magic and I want to feel it too, even if that means forgetting about what happened to me. Even if it means going to hell because of the rituals. I'll worry about the afterlife later. Right now, all I need is to get out of my globe and back out there with Charley, my first friend.

"Don't worry, Joss. I'm fine. We'll all be fine."

I move my wrist and rustle my feather over Charley's. The plumes combine.

♂OSS

I'm going to take Mr. Foster down.

Back at home, locked away in my room, which is high over the street in our converted attic, I'm trying not to smash things. The lamp is what I have my eye on. One nice crack against a wall and that thing will shatter into hundreds of pieces.

Jocelyn, what were you thinking? Dad would ask me, when he saw the damage. *You could have hurt yourself!* Papa Bear would say.

Not the lamp. I pace around. Catch my reflection. My shoulders are hunched up almost near my ears and my jaw is all clenched up. This right here is what The Ravens call my warrior mode. I touch the glass. My flesh finger meets my reflected finger. The mirror is perfectly crackable, though it comes with seven years bad luck.

I step back. Stare into the mirror. Move my hair behind my shoulders. *Jossie, my delicate flower,* Mom always says. When my parents first got divorced, when I was six and Leo was seven, we had no idea what was happening. We only knew that Mom was gone — and then back — twice a month on Sundays. *No, no, Jossie. This movie that we're seeing isn't for you. Too sad.* Her hand on my chin, her hand on my head, and then out the door with my brother.

I move away from the mirror and try to relax my muscles. I won't smash anything. Don't feel like explaining the destruction to either of my parents, who, just like me, have *always* gotten that it's: Enough. Enough. Enough with the news stories. The actors, the politicians, the opera singers, the journalists exposed for assault after years of women silenced. After years of women scared. After years of men, like Caleb, snapping bra straps, telling girls to smile. My parents are ready to fight, all right, but what they've never been ready for is for me to fight with them. To see that I've grown-up. That they've prepared me for this. And sure, maybe I made a mistake. A big, terrible mistake, choosing Charley over Chloe and Mei, but now I know better. Now? I'm ready. Because Brynn too? No.

I open up The Ravens' group text.

I have a plan, I write.

I hit send before I can get scared. Before I can back out.

And though I try not to, I feel it. The anger that I usually try to cool or to shove down or to run away from and which is as old as I am, bubbles through me. Smashing things won't help. Running won't help. Closing my eyes won't help. This time, my rage can't be contained.

•   •   •

Neither of them answers me. I keep waiting and waiting and waiting, but the only texts I get are from Malik. Smileys with hearts for eyes. XOXO's. Cute. I press hearts into a text message beneath the dinner table. Send them back to him.

"Phone away, please," Dad says.

"She doesn't even put it away in the bathroom," Leo says.

Dad, Grandma, Leo, and I sit all spread out at our long table in the dining room, which is big enough to fit ten of us even though there are only four. Grandma doesn't speak. She hasn't spoken since we decided she couldn't live alone anymore, right after the hurricane that tore apart the Jersey Shore. When we picked her up at the house, she carried one beaten-up bag and wore the hurricane in her eyes. It still howls there. It swirls all around in her brown irises. If I could talk to her, I think Grandma would understand me.

"How's work going?" Dad asks Leo.

Dad isn't home on weekends. He's a pharmacist at the hospital, the same one Charley's mom works at. We don't care about his weekend hours, but his guilt is obvious. He uses dinner as his time to interrogate me and my brother. *Are you okay are you happy are you getting enough Vitamin C?*

"Please tell your daughter to be nice to the people I work with." My brother gives me a long look.

Traitor.

"What are you talking about? What happened? What did you do?" Dad leans into Leo. His elbow scrapes his plate.

"*I* didn't do anything. It's her."

"Did you bring your sister to Sebastian's again? We have *talked* about this. You guys. Don't make me take away that car."

"I. Am. Fine. Sebastian's. Is. Fine." My Warrior Mode: Ready to Activate. "Take your arm out of your potatoes. It's disgusting."

"I didn't say you weren't fine. I just don't like you going there. There are plenty of restaurants right here in Raine where the clientele is more —"

"You're the one who taught us that all people are equal. We got that from *you*."

"That's true, Dad. You're actually being like— homophobic right now."

"Homophobic? You're so dumb," I say.

"Something phobic. He's being some kind of phobic."

"Classist? Elitist?" I suggest.

"Yes! That's what I meant. That's what you're being, Dad," Leo says.

My brother, back by my side.

"And besides, you should actually be really proud of me. I totally ghosted this guy Caleb, who was harassing these girls at Sebastian's," I say.

"You... ghosted him?"

I laugh. Catch Grandma's eye. She spears a piece of broccoli. I'm always watching her. Waiting, I guess, for the time to come when she won't remember how to use a fork. For now, I have a feeling she's listening, but I don't know how much she understands.

"Sometimes, it's best to fly under the radar. Ignore, ignore, ignore. Otherwise, who knows what people are going to do? What people are capable of."

"Ghosted literally means ignore. And besides. Are you kidding me? When have you ever ignored anything in your entire life?"

"When you have children—you'll see. It's different."

"Leo was right there. Malik was right there. And even if they *weren't* there —"

"Malik? Are you still hanging out with Malik? In that rental house?"

"No!"

"I think I need to take away that car."

"What?" Leo says to him. "Are you insane? Are you certifiably insane?"

Leo has a way of just saying whatever pops into his head. He's always running his mouth off, except at school, where he sits like a lump in the back of the room slumped down in his chair as far as possible. He didn't apply anywhere but the county college. Pretty sure he doesn't even want to do *that*, but Papa Bear would murder him if he didn't go. That's obvious.

"You cannot go into that house. Not even with your brother there."

"Dad's not insane, by the way." I stand up. Right now, I'm glad for Leo and his stupid mouth. It's easier when it's both of us against Dad. "He's scared."

"You don't know what the world's like. There's a time for activism. There's a time to fight. And there's a time to protect yourself. All I ask—I ask both of you—is that you put yourselves before any cause."

"When have *you* ever done that? When has Mom?"

"Sit down, please. Finish your dinner."

I won't cry because I never cry. Never have, not since I was a little kid and freaked Mom out because I couldn't figure out how to turn the tears off. But now I *do* know how to turn it all off and so while I'll never cry again, I do burn. I grab my phone and get up without pushing in my chair.

I open up Snap and click open a blank message.

I need to talk to you.

Are you okay? Chloe types.

Monday before chorus. Locker room.

You were being really weird after school yesterday, Mei writes. *What's going on?*

I'll tell you Monday.

I plug my phone back in and lay down on my bed. The attic ceiling is arched like a chapel, but I don't pray. I never pray. The only person I believe in is myself.

CHARLEY

The winter sun is white and dazzling, creating ribbons of light over the thinly frozen pond. I don't have our picnic blanket, so I sit right on the ground, inside a circle of sea salt. Daddy's Edgar Allan Poe book lay open, *The Raven* page dog-eared and well-worn. I touch the pages. Embed my fingerprints on the poem, urgently, but tenderly, too, of course, always.

There's a hurricane coming, same as the one that swept Joss's Grandma's home away, dark and looming. I can't escape the feeling. I can't be rid of it, especially not now, Joss's text, *I have a plan,* sitting, unanswered, in my phone. Unfair. Unwarranted. Brynn already admitted she was lying, and that nothing happened yesterday. Joss is now a new Mei, a new Chloe, not a Raven. Not anymore.

"Bring Daddy into this Circle of Safety," I say, my palm tight over his book. "Keep him protected from harm."

I light a tallow candle and it feels good and wise, like I'm a witch of Salem, a pioneer, in kinship with persecuted sisters from ancient times. I wait.

I wait to be filled with stillness, with knowing, for this morning at Brynn's house to be carried away on the wind, Joss's text about my dad swept aside, blown away. Not forgotten, not exactly, just moved, just altered by the breeze and the small flame and the pond and the frosty earth that burrows beneath my clothes and chills me.

The late morning sun is at its full height, its radiant beams touching the trees, coloring the earth, the same light that wakes the seeds and pops the flowers open in spring, the same sun that lit Raine High on fire. I let it touch my face.

And then it happens.

I'm immobile, rooted to the ground like an oak tree, sturdy and wise. I can hear and I can see and I can feel the dirt and the frost and the sun, but I don't move, can't move. I'm dialed in. I've found the frequency. I am of the earth.

Bring Daddy into this Circle of Safety, I think, but don't say, my lips frozen stiff. *Let him know he is protected.*

The shadows dance. But why? How? Nothing moves, nothing stirs, that should cause the shadows to flicker. *Careful*, whispers Air. *Careful, Charley.*

But I don't understand that warning, the same way I don't understand Ava, the car that backed out of my driveway and pulled away. I don't care about the warnings. Not when my power grows every day. Not when the earth knows my name.

•   •   •

Later that day, Daddy takes me bowling. And it's like I'm two people. Charley of the pond and Charley of plain old Raine Hills, good student, book store employee, terrible bowler. I'm good at keeping my identities separate. I'm good at only sharing both versions of Charley with my fellow Ravens. Any other overlap is dangerous. Any other overlap and it's back to being mocked, the skein holding up feathers during chorus, my middle school classmates tripping me in the halls when the teacher's back is turned, the same now as in ancient times, the witches hunted, the witches burned.

Constellations keeps the place dark, with swirling jewel-toned lights that flash on and off on giant screens. The music is terrible and loud and the pizza is cold, but the place feels familiar. Dad and I rent our shoes and put all of our belongings down on the neon purple bench beside our lane. I head straight to the computer while Dad unties his laces.

"I'm going to be Jane Austen today," I say, as I tap J-A-N-E onto the touch screen. "Who are you going to be?"

"Mmmmmm. Orwell?"

"You were Orwell last time!"

"I guess I've been feeling particularly pessimistic lately."

"Pick someone else."

He finishes tying his shoes and joins me at the computer.

"Hemingway?"

"Good."

I finish typing. It's Jane Austen's turn first, so I grab a clementine-colored ball and toss it down the lane. Gutter ball. The same thing happens on my second try. No matter how often we come here, we never improve.

"Nice shot, Jane," Dad says, as the pins reset. "But let's leave this to the master."

Dad gets into a very fancy stance and holds the ball up to his chest like we've seen some of the professionals do. He releases it and knocks down a couple of pins. I feel my whole body relax. After my terrible morning at Brynn's house, a dad and daughter date at Constellations is exactly what I need.

"See? The old warhorse has still got it."

"Can we get pizza? Let's get pizza."

I jab at the touch screen to order food while Dad takes his second turn. It's twenty dollars for a plain pie that will taste like it came out of the fridge instead of the oven. I get Dad the beer he likes and order a soda. The pizza and drinks are our Literary Bowling tradition.

"Jane Austen?" A voice behind me snorts.

The skein.

"Hey, Jane Austen. Hiya, Mr. Hemingway!" a guy from my class says. I don't even know his name. Must have gone to Catholic middle school with Brynn. But Dad will know him.

"Hi, Emma and Julian," Dad says.

"Are we getting our *Macbeth* quizzes back on Monday?" Emma asks.

"It's Saturday," I say. "Why do you want to talk about school on Saturday?"

"You're literally pretending your name is Jane Austen, so I don't think you get to ask me that question."

Emma has hated me for as long as I can remember. *Do you even like boys?* She'd said it over and over, every day, until my hands flew to cover my ears. I didn't like boys. I didn't like girls. Not like *that*. Though I would have liked a friend. I would have loved a friend.

"What are you guys up to?" Dad interrupts.

"Uh… bowling," Julian says. He gestures toward a lane further down the alley, where a bunch of people from my grade are making no attempt to hide that they're staring.

And then I see her: Mei. She's the only one not looking at us. She sits on the bench near her lane, keeping her head down. Hiding from me, probably. I try not to care that she's here, but I feel my cheeks getting hot and I know they're bound to be turning bright pink. It's the cost of being a redhead. All of my emotions show up on my face.

I *like* Mei. That's the hard part. She was better at the rituals than Chloe, Joss, and Brynn. She felt the energy in her gut, same as me. But the lies. And the feathers, the feathers during chorus, in my locker, in my sandwich.

"Well, *anyway*. Have a nice time." Emma turns on her heels and she and Julian saunter back to their friends.

I pick up the ball for my turn, but I'm completely distracted now. I had felt so powerful at the pond this morning, so full and competent. And now? I'm nothing. I'm no one. I watch my classmates form a tight little circle, laughing, while now and then, their eyes wander over to us. Mei stays seated, completely silent. Her friends don't notice that she's upset. Of course, they don't.

Our pizza arrives and Dad and I settle in next to it, lifting the giant, cold slices onto our thin paper plates.

"Culinary masterpiece, as usual, Ms. Austen," Dad says.

I try to give him a little smile, but I don't really mean it and I'm a terrible actor. This isn't fun anymore, though I really want it to be.

"Something the matter?"

I open my mouth to say something, but nothing comes out. I take a bite of pizza instead and sneak another look at my classmates, who pretend to shriek while Julian mimes dropping a bowling ball on his foot.

"You don't want to be like them," Dad says. "You won't know that until you're older, but I promise, you'll appreciate who you are once you're out of high school."

I've heard that speech so many times that I have it memorized. First, things were going to be better in high school. But now that I'm in high school, things will be better in college. I don't even need to listen to know what Dad will say next, so I only half look at him and half turn my attention back to my classmates. Emma catches my eye and waves and then whispers something to Julian and Mei. Julian laughs, but Mei doesn't. She looks startled. She looks—anticipatory. She looks—determined. My God, what is she going to do?

I try to focus on Dad.

"For a minimalist, Mr. Hemingway, you have a lot to say."

Dad laughs and spits out some of his beer.

"You're so smart. My best girl."

Out of the side of my eye, I see Mei get up. I see her walking slowly toward us, like a lion stalking its prey.

Go away.

I have the instinct to step in front of Dad like I'm shielding him from a bullet. Mei comes closer. Closer.

Go away, you traitor. Snitch. Liar.

The anger courses through me. It fills me like I'm rooted, that oak tree again, sucking in the energy of everyone around me. She's two feet away. The energy pops. It sizzles, electric.

"Charley," Mei says. Her voice is bitter. Icy.

"Hey, Mei," Dad says.

"Are you —"

No. You will not hurt him.

Somewhere, suddenly, an electronic whir. The lights at Constellations spark, grow brighter, and then we're plummeted into darkness.

"What happened?" Dad asks. "What on earth?"

And it's greater than Air rustling through the skein's sheet music. And it's greater than the Raven and the construction paper, scattered across Brynn's floor. This is light, electricity, current. There are confused mutters everywhere. Cell phones pulled from pockets, flashlights and screens lighting up the dark. A backup generator revs and purrs and periphery emergency lights flicker on all across the bowling alley.

"Whoa! This is crazy!" I hear Julian say. Mei runs back to her friends, her way lit by phone. Mei in retreat. Mei — gone.

"Sorry, everyone. Sorry, you guys," a manager, young, walks from lane to lane. "We don't know — have it up and running in a few —"

"This is boring anyway," Emma's voice pops out above the rest. "Let's go, you guys."

"So weird," Dad says to me. He puts his arm around my shoulders. His laughter and his touch rush through me.

It's not weird. It's energy. It's power.

I stand there with his arms wrapped around me. He might think he's protecting me—though, from what? The dark? The sudden illumination of emergency exit signs? The undercurrent of electricity that tries to burst back on? But there is nothing he needs to protect me from. I'm the one protecting him. This is the spell's work, the spell I did this afternoon at the pond. And I did it on my own, without Mei or Chloe. Without even Brynn or Joss.

I'm so angry with them, with all of them, for almost letting them ruin *this*—Dad's arm around me, his laughter, loud and bright. His glowing pride for me, over the only other thing that I'm good at in this world: books.

The lights burst back on as quickly as they'd disappeared. The lanes reset, the pins lifted and placed back down again with metal claws.

"We're back!" the manager says. Like we didn't know. Like it wasn't obvious that the afternoon, like the lanes, has been reset. Rewound. That history has been changed, crisis averted, energy captured and channeled because of me. Charley Foster. Reader. Writer. Witch.

"You're up, Ernest," I say.

The lights change colors — lime green to aqua, to amethyst.

"Thank you, Jane."

The pins fall. The afternoon fades into night.

ʙRYNN

The cursor blinks at me, but I'm too distracted to write anything. I know that Mr. Foster wants us to start our *Macbeth* essays with a "hook" — something that will catch the reader's attention. But all I can think of is the word *why. Why, why, why, why?*

I type the word out many times. I type a whole paragraph of whys. I bold them. I jack the font up to sixteen. And that's it. That's as far as I can go. Normally, I'd call Charley. She always helps me with English homework, but obviously, *so* obviously, that's out of the question right now.

And even if I can revise it, how will I get it to Mr. Foster? Just show up at his classroom door alone? Take Joss with me and risk her going into full on warrior mode? After Charley and I had completely ignored Joss's texts last night, she'd sent another two this morning.

"I'll do this with or without you."

And a few minutes later:

"This is the year we rise."

What do these texts mean? Why didn't she just believe me when I said I made everything up? Or worse, worse, why *did* Charley believe me when I'd said I made everything up?

My fingers tighten at the computer keys. They tingle and then lock into fists.

I'm such an outsider. Even with my best friends, my only friends, I'm still the puzzle piece that's not exactly the right shape to click in with the rest.

I can't breathe.

I crawl out of my desk chair and curl up into a ball on the floor.

My curtains are watching me. My bed is staring at me.

There isn't enough air in the room.

"Mommy!" I yell. "Mommy!"

I hear her feet on the stairs, and she's in my room in a flash. She sits down next to me on the floor and puts her hand on top of my hair. "Do you want a yellow pill?"

That's what we call them. Yellow pills. Like I'm a five-year-old.

"Remember, you have too much air in your lungs. Not too little," Mommy says. She stole this line from a nurse who said it to me during one of our multiple ER visits. Mommy should probably cite that or she'll be accused of plagiarism like me. Turns out, plagiarism comes at a high, high cost here in Raine Hills. "Should we call Daddy? Or do you think we need to go to the hospital?"

News flash: there is literally nothing the hospital can do for a panic attack except make you feel stupid for wasting their time when someone next to you is actually sick. Mommy should know that by now.

"Can you tell me what caused this? Is it my mammogram? Should I get a paper bag?"

"You're asking too many questions."

"I'm sorry. I'm really sorry. It's just hard to watch. Makes me feel helpless."

I feel helpless too. The room is spinning. It's flying around like I'm watching a carousel ride in a dream. Mr. Foster's hands come at me and then spin away again. Mommy's scan rises and dips. The raven appears, laughing from a tree.

"Did something happen?" Mommy can't help herself with the questions.

"Just the mammogram, I guess."

"You know that you have to take very slow breaths. Inhale and count to four."

I lean into the warmth of her. She smells like cinnamon candy.

Willow sneaks in the door. Plops himself on her lap. We're all obsessed with Mommy. Every last one of us.

"Now exhale and count to four."

"I think I'm dying."

"You're not dying. And you know what? I'm not either. I'm not going anywhere. I've been praying. I think that God is going to take care of me. And us."

"Okay," I say. Because that's all I've got.

"And I'm sure you're praying, too. In your own way."

"Yeah, in my way."

I just can't tell her what way that actually is. It's true that she's open about a lot of things. Her ideas about people and what's fair and what's right are the same ideas as most people in Raine. Somehow, she balances modern life with Catholic life. But witchcraft? Finding out that we're doing spells for her? That will be the line in the sand.

"Let's Facetime Daddy," she says.

I pick up my phone and hand it to her as a shiver runs through my whole body. Mommy leans over Willow and hugs me. She is warm and good and smart and mine. But she can't help me with this. Neither of my parents can.

Daddy picks up. He always does, as long as he's between clients. He appears on my screen, leaned way back in his big armchair. One look at me and he knows.

"Yellow pill?" he asks.

"She doesn't want it."

"Distraction, then," Daddy says. "Brynnie Brynn, let's get the other side of your brain working. Sing a song?"

Singing has always been the way to bring me back to myself. My parents and The Ravens are the only ones on this earth who know about that because I can't get myself to sing by myself in public. But concerts for the shampoo and body wash? Always sold out.

"What should we sing? A little Row, Row Your Boat? We can do it in rounds."

"Oh my God, Daddy."

But he's off and away already, with fake paddles and all. Mommy joins him. They're a hot mess express. I mean, let's pick a key here.

"Careful, Daddy. What if your clients hear you?"

"White noise machines."

"There aren't enough white noise machines in the *world*..."

"Hey, you."

"Feeling better?" Mommy asks.

Yes, and no. No, and yes.

"I don't know," I say. And that's the real truth. The carousel circles again. I see his hands. I remember the circuits in my brain burning, *pop, pop,* one by one. Watching from the ceiling and from my own eyes at the same time. If I could tell them... if I could only tell them... but that's impossible.

Daddy sings louder. Mommy holds me close.

"Take another breath. One, two, three, four."

I do it. I breathe.

"She's okay now," Mommy says to Daddy. "I've got it from here."

They give each other a look through the phone, like *we'll talk about this later*. They think I don't see it or that I'm still too young to understand.

"Mommy," I say, after Daddy hangs up. And I want that word to just mean *everything*, but of course it doesn't. "Why am I so different?"

"How do you mean?"

"I told you that Charley and Joss…" I choose my words carefully. "They can always tell what I'm feeling. But I can't tell what they're feeling. Why not?"

"Is that what's got you panicked?" Mommy laughs. The sound is so large that it fills the room. Startles Willow. "I'm going to tell you a secret."

I lean in to her. The cinnamon is close.

"They're faking."

I smile a little. Mommy's got it all twisted around. She looks up at my open computer and my bold 'whys' stare out at us both. "Why what?"

"Oh, like—why do I have to write this stupid essay about this stupid book?"

"*Macbeth* is a play, not a book."

"Now you sound like Charley."

"Why don't you give her a call if you're struggling with it? Maybe she can come over."

"Maybe if I just think really hard, *Charley, please come over here*, she'll get the message. I think she has ESP."

"Or you can just text her." Mommy kisses the top of my head and leans her back against my bed with her palms on my rug. "Hey, what's this?" She pulls something out from just underneath my bed.

Charley's quartz. She must have left it here after yesterday morning's ritual.

"From Charley," I say. "A present."

"Pretty." She hands it to me and stands up before crossing to the door. "Are you feeling any better?"

"Little bit."

She pauses in my doorway and then turns back around.

"There are witches in *Macbeth*, right?"

My breath catches again, but I recover and try to make my voice as casual as possible. "It's not actually in English, so I'm not a hundred percent sure."

"Are you reading this for school? Or did Charley ask you to read it?"

"Charley's *dad* asked me to read it. It's definitely for school." At the mention of Mr. Foster, I start sweating. "Why are you asking?"

"Sometimes I think," she pauses and puts two fingers on my door frame. "Charley doesn't practice witchcraft, does she?"

"*What*?"

"I just wondered if maybe that's what the three of you —"

"No, Mommy. We're just regular friends." I'm going to *become* my panic. Does Mommy feel the healing spells we've been doing? "Why do you ask?"

"Oh, I don't know. She's just so… earthly. But then completely off-centered at the same time. And then you always talk about this ESP thing."

"She's not off-centered! That's just as bad as what everyone says about her at school."

"I didn't mean to offend. Just had to ask. What you do on your own time is your business, but as I'm sure you know, I don't want any of that in my house."

"I know."

More Lies.

"I don't ask you to go to church, but I do ask that you respect me."

"I do."

"Good."

She disappears down the hall. I leap up, shut my bedroom door, run back to my computer, and open up the search engine.

Does God hate witches? I type.

The paper will have to wait.

CHARLEY

Early Monday morning, before chorus, the halls are silent. Deadly still. Dad's classroom door is locked. I hadn't counted on that, but it doesn't matter. I'll create a protective barrier right outside the door. If Joss tries to enact any kind of *plan* at school, Dad will be safe from harm.

I dig into my backpack and pull out a pentacle charm from Ava and two makeup compacts. I flip them open and stand them, facing each other, in front of Dad's classroom door. The tiny mirrors stare at each other like long-ago enemies in a duel. I put a candle between them and pull out a cigarette lighter. It catches, and I put it to the wick. The candle flickers, its reflection caught in the double mirrors. It's pretty, such light in the dim hall.

"Whatever Joss puts out into the universe comes back to her instead," I whisper. "Whatever energy Jocelyn Esposito sets forth is instead reflected back."

I could get in real trouble for this. I know it, deep in my gut. But I have role models. The girls of *The Crucible* or Hester Prynne and her bright red A. Heroes, all. Persecuted. Blamed. I can be like them. A woman ahead of her time.

"May Joss's energy reverse and strike her instead."

It's not black magic. Not really, not exactly. There are so many shades of colors, so much space in between the labels *good* and *evil*. Why doesn't anyone ever focus on that space? Only the writers do. Only the poets do, dreaming up colors beside an apple tree, imagining the right word for core, the right color to describe the skin, the exact shade, so different from, so much subtler, from, plain old *red*.

Do no harm. And I'm not. This is a different shade, a lighter hue than *harm*. I'm not creating any new energy, any new power—just Joss's own intentions, swung back around to her. It's easy. It's simple. It's right. Isn't it?

I don't know. I don't know anything. I've stopped blogging. My *Book of Shadows*, all posted online for others to see (because why not? We are witches of the modern age) has gone completely silent. I've lost my way. A ship, alone at sea.

I love my dad.

That's the truth I hold in my stomach. My book-reading Dad. *The Very Hungry Caterpillar* or *Goodnight Moon* over and over and over, beneath the covers, with a flashlight, while Mom was on an overnight shift or while Mom slept off another angry, silent dinner.

Dad and Charley. Charley and Dad.

It's okay to cry. That's the wisdom of the women in books. Their secret weeping. Their hidden pain. I touch a tear with one finger and put it to the pentacle. I don't know why. Read nothing about tears or pinkies or pentacles, only know what I sense, what I feel, am guided by that, like footprints that follow the edge of the tide.

There's a sudden slamming sound from down the hall. I freeze but then recover. Blow out the candle and shove it back in my bag, not even checking that it'd cooled or even gone all the way out. I pick up the mirrors. Hold them both in my hands just as two people push through a door down the hall and head toward the gym. They don't see me, but I see them. Their shadows dart over the walls in the early morning light that creeps in through the courtyard windows.

Their voices rise. Nervous laughter. Mei and Chloe. I'd know them anywhere. What are they doing here so early? Where are they going? I stand up. Drop the pentacle to the ground. It's not wet. The tear now dried. It's my mark. I was here. I'm *here*.

They're up to something. They all are. I follow them down the hall.

♪OSS

I pace around the empty locker room. I open and close random doors and check Snap every three seconds for messages from Mei or Chloe. They should be here by now. Chorus is going to start in twenty minutes and there's a lot to say. There's a lot to plan out.

Last Thursday, which was only four days ago, Charley had stood in this exact spot waving her feather in the air. *This is our year,* she'd said. *This is the year we rise.* And now, check this out: I'm the only Raven here. The only Raven rising.

The anger seizes me up, and it's either punch something or run, but the locker room door swings open and I shake my shoulders loose.

Mei and Chloe arrive together. Mei wears long earrings that catch in her dark hair. She touches the jewelry as they come closer and put their bags down on the long bench.

"We made it!" Chloe's eyes always look like they have jokes in them. I remember that from our seventh-grade sleepovers. "You should be very proud of us. Getting here so early on a Monday morning."

"Doesn't feel early to me, but I go to bed at ten and get up at six."

"Senior citizen."

"She's sundowning. At age seventeen."

Mei keeps one hand through the loop of the handle on her bag. Her words are friendly enough, but the look on her face reminds me of Brynn's cat when he shows me his belly. If I pet Willow a second too long, I'm going to get clawed. Just like Willow, Mei's sizing me up.

"Thanks for meeting me. I know it's super early."

Chloe sits down on the bench. "No, it's fine. I mean... just because Charley kicked us out... I don't see why *we* can't talk and stuff."

"That's what I wanted to... I feel really, really bad about this summer. And I hoped we could —"

"We just don't understand what happened. Why would you pick Charley over us? We've been friends since sixth grade. You only started hanging out with Charley two years ago."

"It was very, very stupid and I'm really, really sorry."

"And we're sorry about the feathers," Chloe says. "We didn't mean for it to hurt *you*. Or Brynn."

"I mean, I get it, I guess. Now I do, anyway."

"Is that really what you wanted to tell us? That you're sorry?" Mei asks.

"No, it's—it's more than that. Listen. I have some information."

"Will this information explain why you were being so weird on Friday after school?"

"I think so?"

"What, then?"

"You guys." I pause, take a deep breath, and then spit it out all at once. "You're not the only victims."

There's a really awkward silence. I swear it lasts like a full thirty seconds. I don't know whose turn it is to talk. Don't know the rules for this kind of thing.

"*Survivors,*" Mei breaks the silence. "Not victims."

"Yes! Survivors. That's what I meant. You're not the only survivors. There are more."

"You?" Chloe whispers.

"Is that why you were being so weird on Friday?"

"No, no. Not me."

"Who then?" Mei pauses. Then her face lights up and I know she knows.

"Brynn. Yeah, it's Brynn," I say to her. "But she doesn't—she isn't—she told Charley it didn't happen."

"But it did?"

"It did."

"Poor Brynn," Chloe says. "Oh, no."

"What does this have to do with you, then? Where is *she*?" Mei asks. "You shouldn't be telling us this without her permission."

"I have a plan."

I stand up straighter. Superhero strong. Warrior strong.

"We're not doing magic anymore. Me and Chloe. So, if that's what —"

"Oh, God, no. I'm not… I miss how it was in eighth grade. We never needed spells or feathers or whatever in middle school. Before The Ravens, it was just… us. And the feelings. I don't know what I believe about magic or any of that. But I do know that we can't just sit around doing nothing. We have to stop Mr. Foster before he can hurt anyone else. That's just plain old doing what's right. It's justice."

"Why should we believe you want to help now? We told Charley, and she did nothing." Mei stares straight ahead. She looks like she's talking to the locker behind me instead of to me. "She called us liars. And you took her side."

And it's like that mirror? The magical one I always ask Malik to look into to see our future? It's suddenly swung back around and pointing toward me, except it's not my future I see in there. It's just me. Plain old me. And I hate who I see.

"I guess… I didn't want to believe it. Deep down. You know. That it could be true. That my friend's dad would do something like this. When I was growing up, my parents were always fighting *something,* and I honestly hated it. It scared me. That the world was so terrible. Not that that's a good excuse. But I put up this shield. Blocked things out. Pretended to myself that it wasn't true. But even while I did that, I didn't want Charley to kick you out. I argued with her about it all the time. Promise."

"Arguing with her doesn't mean you didn't side with her. Arguing with her was just your guilty conscience. You know that, right?"

"I'm trying to fix it."

"She's doing dark magic now. Or at the least, gray magic. Did you know that? Don't you still hang out with her all the time?"

"No. Do no harm. Charley would never. And *gray* magic? What even is that?"

"How do you not know this? Magic falls along a continuum. Like a scale. White magic is only used for good purposes. It's what the first Raven tenet means: Do no harm. Black magic is what most people think of when they think of witches. Spells used for evil or selfish reasons or even calling on demons or spirits. And then there's Charley. Who, I think, right now, is falling in the middle. Gray magic. Extending her will over someone, even if she thinks it's for a good reason."

"She's not doing that."

"Oh, no. She *is.* It happened at the bowling alley. I was there. I *saw* her doing it," Mei continues. "I went over to her. Even though her dad was there, I walked over to her, anyway. Even after she called us liars and kicked us out, and even though I knew she probably wouldn't talk to me after the feather thing, I just felt like she needed me. She seemed so sad. I felt it from across the room. But as I got closer? The look on her face? I was *scared* of Charley. And then the lights went out. Seconds later. No way that wasn't related. And gray magic is just a stepping stone. Don't you see? She's moving her way along the continuum. And she's getting good at it."

"The lights went out? Anything could cause that."

"No," Mei says. "No. I have studied this. I have—honestly, I've practiced way more than you ever did. And way more than you know that I have. You haven't talked to us in months. You don't know us anymore. Not really."

"Why should we trust you?" Chloe breaks in.

"Because I believe you."

"Yeah, okay."

"Well, not about the magic stuff. But I mean—about what happened to you."

"Well, that's good, Joss." Mei says. "That at least… it's a start. Because you have no idea."

"Tell me, then. I want to understand. What happened to you? What did he do?"

Chloe looks at Mei. Mei nods at her, like *you can tell Joss if you want.* I remember being part of that. Being able to look at them and just know what they were thinking, this really cool silent language where we never needed words.

"He said he needed to conference with me."

"That's what he did to Brynn!"

"Let her talk, Joss," Mei says.

"I'm sorry. I'm sorry."

"I sat down next to him on top of his desk. You know how he sits up there. And we started going over my test grades when he sort of like…" Chloe squeezes her eyes up super tight, like she's trying to squirt the memory out of her brain. "He put his hand up my skirt."

"Oh my God."

"She's not done."

"He kissed me. I can still like—I can't wash it off. On my neck. Like his disgusting lips are *still* there."

"I am so, so sorry. I had no idea that that—Oh my God."

"I ran away. I jumped off the desk and ran out. He didn't chase me, though I thought maybe he was, so I just kept running, until I found Mei and—I don't know what he would have done if I hadn't run away. I don't know what he did to Brynn or what he's done to others at school. What does he do to girls who don't run away?"

"You were so strong to run. You did the exact right thing," Mei says quickly.

"Chloe. I don't even know what to say. Have you tried to tell anyone else? Besides Charley, I mean."

"Like the *principal?* Ms. Suarez? Are you kidding?" Mei says. "She'd never believe it. That's why we went to Charley! If *Charley* tells Ms. Suarez the truth about her dad, then Ms. Suarez will have no choice but to listen."

"I told Mrs. Miller," Chloe says.

"What?" Mei turns to her. "You didn't tell me this."

"But Mrs. Miller must be friends with Mr. Foster. She just said he's a good man. That I'm getting all hyped up from the media. That everyone is getting all riled up and witch —" she cuts herself off.

"Witch hunting," I finish.

"He did it to me, too. Not as dramatic as what happened to Chloe, but still. It was absolutely awful. He picks on the quiet ones. But it's just our word against his. Mrs. Miller loves him. Principal Suarez loves him. All the teachers do. He's been here forever. He's a freaking institution," Mei says.

"That's exactly why I wanted to talk to you. I have a plan, but I need your help."

Mei looks down at the floor. Deep in thought. Calculating, thinking before she talks. Finally, she asks, "What do you want us to do?"

"Mr. Foster—he tutors SAT after school. We'll get him alone there. We'll set a trap."

"A trap? What, like use one of us as bait?"

"Not you. Not *you*. Me."

"You are so stupid." Mei stands up. "Come on, Chloe."

But Chloe doesn't get up. She opens her mouth to say something and her words are unusually quiet for someone normally so bright and sunny. She's barely loud enough for me to hear her. Reminds me of Brynn. Not strong.

"It's not a game," Chloe whispers. "If he touches you, you will never be the same. You will never be the same ever again. You need to slow down. Think about what you're doing."

"There's no time to slow down! There's so much anger in me that's bursting to get out. Like I could *punch* something right now and not even feel it, I swear."

Mei grabs both her bag and Chloe's.

"Let me help. Let this be how I help."

"*No.*" Mei pulls Chloe up by one arm. Chloe's crying so hard that she's lost her balance. In a move that is very un-me, I reach out to hug Chloe. "Don't touch her." Mei pulls Chloe toward the door. She tugs it open and yanks Chloe through it. It slams shut behind them.

Okay.

Calm breaths. Shield up. Strong.

I'll fix it.

But even so. Even still. I've never failed at anything the way I just failed at this.

There's not time to relive it. No time to think, because the locker room door swings open again.

"Charley."

Her face is paler than usual. She looks like a ghost, except for the black circles under her eyes. She's dressed differently, too. Wearing all black. No pops of colored socks sticking out of her boots.

"I won't let you," she finally says. "You won't win."

"Charley —"

But she doesn't let me explain anything. Just spins around and leaves as quickly as she came in. The locker room goes silent. The whole school is quiet. My breathing is the only noise.

ẞRYNN

Years ago, before any of us set foot in this place, some artsy kids drew a giant Raine High Hurricane mural over the bleachers in our gym/auditorium. Some days I think the mural's cool. Today, I think it's depressing. It's bad enough to live in a town with the word "rain" in it. It's worse to think of hurricanes. Especially with what happened at the beach to Joss's Grandma.

Charley and I never answered Joss's texts, so now I don't know if Joss's mad at us or not. It's making me extra anxious, because I really need Joss's help. I didn't re-write my paper. I don't know if Mr. Foster will tell Ms. Suarez about the plagiarism or worse. So, so much worse.

The panic is grabbing out for me. No. No. No. The skein girls already think I'm a complete freak. Not here, please, God.

But after all my reading last night, I know God wants nothing to do with me. I read a Catholic website that says that even if a witch doesn't worship the devil, just doing a ritual opens people up to evil spirits or demonic possession. After I found that, I closed out the website and hid my computer in a desk drawer beneath the construction paper. The construction paper that is probably cursed now from Charley's spell.

Imagine Father Dooley could see me now? Father Dooley used to dress up like Santa Claus at our second-grade Christmas fair. One time he let me tug his beard to show me it wasn't real when I was too scared to sit on his lap. Or Sister Rose, who worked in our school library and once dug through shelves of books to find *Madeline* for me, even though I was too shy to ask for it. I've failed all of them. I've failed Mommy most of all.

My fingers get sweaty and create thumbprints on my sheet music. All around me, my classmates practice for our winter concert like the end of the world isn't happening. Like the ceiling isn't about to cave in on us.

Should old acquaintance be forgot, and never brought to mind?

I am going to choke to death right in front of them. I grip on to Charley's sleeve.

Should old acquaintance be forgot,
And auld lang syne?

She looks at me for a second like, *what?* And then goes right back to singing. She's in a terrible mood today. Looks like she hasn't slept in days, either.

I'm sick. I feel so, so sick.

Maybe I need my pill. Maybe I need a few. But *no. Stop thinking about that.*

"Charley, please." But she's not looking at me at all. No one is. Not even Mrs. Miller, who is focused on the piano. Instead of answering me, Charley's looking at something on the top riser. A few of the skein girls follow her eyes. Then they whisper and point and I'm sure they've brought their feathers again. I turn around to see and quickly understand that whatever everyone's looking at has nothing to do with me.

One by one, all the chorus girls drop their music to their sides and stare at Chloe, who's crouched down on the top riser. It reminds me of what I must have looked like two years ago, when Charley and Joss took me out into the hallway and I told them that Mommy was sick.

Charley, I tug on her sleeve. *I can't breathe.* But she isn't paying any attention to me. How typical. Not unusual. A Day in the Life of Brynn Madeline McLaughlin.

Mei puts her hand on Chloe's back. Mei and Chloe, Chloe and Mei. Bonded even closer together now because… because…

"Mrs. Miller," Emma calls out. "Mrs. Miller, please help."

The piano stops. Mrs. Miller gets up from the bench and rushes over to the risers.

"Chloe?" she asks. "Chlo, are you sick?"

I'm sick. I'm sick, too.

But no one cares. No one sees.

Sometimes I think I'm ignored because I'm quiet. Most of the time, I think I'm ignored because I'm the biggest wreck of a person who has ever gone to Raine High and no one has time to notice me.

If being ignored is part of God's punishment, then fine. If it's part of my penalty for the rituals, then okay. I let go of Charley's arm. *You can breathe,* I tell myself. *Count to four.*

"Come down, please," Mrs. Miller says. "Mei, please help Chloe get down."

Mei takes one of Chloe's arms and Emma takes the other. They bring her down one level at a time. When they get to the bottom, Joss doesn't make room to let them through. Mei shoves her a little, and Joss looks surprised. What's happening? What's going on? Why is the world crumbling down?

Mrs. Miller leads Chloe out into the hallway. Mei and Emma follow behind. The risers explode in whispers.

"Charley, Charley, I can't breathe," I say.

"You can. You really, *really* can."

She doesn't say it nicely. She doesn't say it with patience. She says it like the doctors do in the ER. Charley stares at the auditorium door long after it has swung shut. She keeps looking at it even after Chloe's crying becomes distant and then disappears.

"What did you *do?*" she yells out to Joss. "What did you do to them this morning?"

Suddenly, I understand. Joss's plan.

There shouldn't be a plan about this. There shouldn't be any kind of plan when it comes to a man, his fingers, my zipper. There are only feelings. Only shame that pumps, pumps, pumps. A dark hole, trying to crawl out of it, a ceiling, flesh colors, flying, falling. Everything is my fault. *I'm sorry, God. I'm sorry for the rituals. But please don't let him hurt me anymore.*

I'm so dizzy.

The world has gone crazy. The hurricane walls come close. The hurricane walls close in on me.

"Charley," I say. "I feel —"

The auditorium goes black.

CHARLEY

I don't know how hard Brynn has hit her head. She's probably only been unconscious now for about ten seconds, but it feels like an eternity. There are no adults around. Mrs. Miller has gone off with Chloe and Mei.

The skein stares at me. They stare at me so hard; it feels like they're shooting lasers that bore holes in my skin. Do they know? About the candle and the mirrors and the tear from this morning?

"What happened?" Khadija asks. Like she cares about Brynn. Like she deserves to know. "We need to get Mrs. Miller."

"Khadija, Brynn just faints a lot — hang on —" Joss yells out, but Khadija bounds off of the risers and disappears into the hall. Like Joss should be the one protecting Brynn. This is all her fault in the first place.

"Aren't you going to do something?" Joss yells up to me now. She runs up the platforms, the skein parting for her as she reaches each new level. When she gets to us, she bends down and starts shaking Brynn.

"She doesn't want *you*," I manage to say.

"Okay... but you're literally not doing anything!"

That's true enough. I crouch down with Joss. Brynn's eyes are wide open, but I can tell she doesn't see us.

"Use your feather!" a voice calls out. There's some awkward laughter, and then back to silence. Not even the lights, which usually hum all around us, make a sound.

Twenty seconds gone. Joss and I shake Brynn wildly.

"Brynn," Joss says over and over. "Brynn, get up, girl."

"What are we going to do?"

"She'll be okay, Charley. Just wait and see."

But Joss doesn't understand. I meant: Just — what are we going to do — about everything?

Brynn blinks, shakes her head, and then looks from me to Joss, to me again. "What happened?" she whispers from the ground.

"You fainted," Joss and I say at the same time.

"She okay?" someone asks.

"How's your head?"

"Am I bleeding? I don't think I'm bleeding."

"We've got to go to the office. You've got to go home. Can you stand?" I pull Brynn up to a sitting position. She looks wobbly and unsure, but she's awake.

"Don't move her. Khadija's coming back with Mrs. Miller," Joss says.

"Do you *see* Khadija or Mrs. Miller?"

"Charley!" Brynn says, "Please. Joss is —"

I can't be here when Mrs. Miller comes back. Mei and Chloe could, right now, right this very second, be telling her all kinds of things about my dad. Was *this* Joss's plan? To have Chloe cry to get Mrs. Miller's attention?

My legs have a sudden kick in them. I want to run and run and run and never stop moving until I find somewhere safe to go. Maybe I can find a farmhouse in the middle of the country somewhere, where I'd tend to the chickens and milk the cow and live off of the beauty of the land. There'd be no threats there but the occasional Kansas tornado, which is an act of God, not man, and therefore, somehow, feels less terrible. It feels like the natural order of things, the wrath of the spinning earth. I understand the earth. I'm connected to the sky. It's people that are impossible.

"Let me help you!" Joss says.

I make Brynn stand. Joss gathers the fallen sheet music and Brynn's bag, but I take both from her hands. "I got it."

"You can't carry all of that and help her."

"I said I got it."

I'm not stupid. Most people—even Joss, apparently think that my head is up in the clouds, that I'm floating around up there with the smoke of blown-out ritual candles. But actually, the only thing I am in this world is smart. And because I'm smart, because I've read more books than anyone else in this school, probably even more than Dad, and because the feelings of every person in this gym flow freely into me, just about knocking me to my knees, I know Chloe was crying this morning because of something Joss did. I might not know exactly what she said to Chloe and Mei, but I know Joss has done something that has the power to hurt me more than the dozens of birthday parties where my classmates called me a freak, more than all the teasing at the bookstore.

I guide Brynn down the risers and onto the gym floor. The skein's laser eyes stare.

I see Brynn look back at Joss and shrug. Even that small glance between them is a betrayal. *Charley's gone off the deep end this time*, they say with their eyes. If they think I don't know what's happening here, then they don't understand me at all. I know everything. I see everything.

"Don't go with her, Brynn!" I hear one of the skein girls say as Brynn and I push through the auditorium doors.

"*Witch*," whispers another.

"Leave Charley alone," Joss says.

And that small act of kindness nearly kills me.

•   •   •

"I think Joss talked to Mei and Chloe this morning. I think that's why Chloe was crying," Brynn says as we walk toward the office.

"Of course, that's why Chloe was crying."

"I want you to know that I would never do that. I would never hurt you." I feel Brynn's body slacken, and I tighten my grip on her waist. "You're my best friend," she continues. "And I want us to always be friends. No matter what happens."

"Do you think Mei and Chloe told Mrs. Miller about the rumors? I saw them here at school really early this morning. With Joss. Do you think that was Joss's plan?" I ask.

Brynn is quiet for a very, very long time. I used to think I had to repeat things to her, since she takes so long to respond to questions. But after a year or so, I realized Brynn isn't like me and Joss, who have quick answers on our tongues.

"They're such liars," Brynn finally says, but her voice is so soft, I can barely hear her. We take a few more steps before she breaks away from me. "I'm sorry you're going through this."

Oh, finally. Oh, thank you, sweet friend. I take the words in. I hold them close. For a few seconds, I feel a sense of stillness, an absolute calm, like I've reached that barn in Kansas, like we are surrounded by sweet hay and bees carrying pollen on their tiny black legs.

"Charley, why is this happening?"

"Why is what happening?"

"I've been reading a lot about…" Brynn trails off. "Do you think God's mad at us? Because of the Ravens."

"There's no such thing as God."

"How do you know?"

"I—I don't. I don't know anything. You shouldn't listen to me. About anything."

"Are we… *bad* witches?

"Of course, not."

But I don't know. I don't know. I don't know.

I never *meant* to be bad. Does that count for something? It must. In all the books I've read, or, at least, in most of the books I've read, even if the protagonist does something questionable, there's a reason. There's usually a really *good* reason for her actions.

What's mine?

Is it really black or white? Am I wrong about the gray? The shades in between?

Must I be all good or all evil? And if so, am I the protagonist or the antagonist here? The victim or the hero?

"We're good witches," I say. Because how could we be anything but that? "Like, just now, when you said you were sorry for what I was going through? I felt this —- stillness all around us. There's this energy that's just hanging here, waiting to be tapped. Waiting for us to reach out to it and direct it toward goodness."

"But toward goodness how? How can we know what's good and what isn't?"

"I know that your mom's test is going to be fine on Friday. I know that it's because we helped her. I'm not sure about God. I don't know about any of that. I just trust what I feel, which is a very good, very calm energy around us." I pause. "The energy grows every day. The power... don't you feel it, too?"

"I do," Brynn says quickly.

"They're always going to come for us, you know. People have been hunting witches for centuries. But that's not God, that's people. People are scared of us because they know we can sense who they really are. No one wants to be confronted with a mirror. That's why you—well, that's why you lied, isn't it? You couldn't own up that you had plagiarized that paper. It was easier to shift the blame."

"I'm sorry I lied."

"I'm not mad. I'm not mad at all, because I know my dad. I know he's a good man. I know he would never do that to you."

I don't mention the way Brynn's text, *Charley, can we talk?* runs through my head on repeat, the way I hear it at night, the way I hear it in the shower, the way I had typed it up in my blog and then discarded the draft as quickly as I'd written it.

"I'm so, so sorry I lied. I'm so sorry that like- I feel like I can't breathe."

"Hey, hey. We can't have you fainting again, right? I've got you. I'm right here."

But that stillness? The barn house from just a few seconds ago? The more we talk, the further away it feels.

I might be very good at witchcraft. I might be getting better at it every day.

But I'm a terrible person.

I'm a terrible friend.

I know this. I feel it in my bones.

"Thank you so much for being my friend," Brynn says, between deep breaths. "I know that I'm a lot to handle. And I'm just so grateful —"

"Come on," I say, taking her hand back in mine. "Let's go to the office."

We turn a corner and head into the main corridor. Raine High is set a way back from Main Street, on a quiet block belonging only to the school. The windows of this corridor face front, where those tall, yellowing willow trees dip toward the sidewalk.

"Looks like the trees are crying," I say.

"That's why they're called weeping willows, isn't it?"

"Oh, yeah. I forgot. Too bad I didn't patent that," I say, when we nearly crash straight into Dad.

"Well, well, well. Fancy meeting you here," he says.

"Dad!" I say, as Brynn's body goes stiff.

"Cutting first period?" He laughs.

Brynn backs up and stands behind me, using my body as a shield.

She's trembling. I feel her entire body shaking behind me. It's impossible to pretend something like this — this *terror* that rolls out of her like waves in high tide, pushed, pulled, by the moon.

I'm going to throw-up.

She wasn't lying. I feel it. I know.

"Where you off to?"

"Office," I choke out. "She's… sick."

Standing there like that, with Dad in front of me, and Brynn behind me, I suddenly understand something I should have known since I got Brynn's text, but that I haven't let myself know until now. I'm going to have to pick. I'm going to have to choose between Dad and my best friend.

"Sorry to hear that," Dad says.

Tell me what to do. I want to scream toward the sun, toward the stars, toward the moon that must still hang, must still dangle there, hidden behind the piercing blue of a winter morning. And even now, knowing all this, understanding all this, I still gravitate toward him. Pulled like that tide. Why aren't my spells working? Why can't I protect him from this?

I see it. A premonition. A warning. The handcuffs. The bars. Dad gone. Just me and Mom, alone, angry, the house quiet, the house bereft.

"Is there something I can do?" he asks.

Brynn's entire body quivers, curled tightly behind mine.

The energy bursts. The farmhouse is gone, plucked up into the vortex of a tornado.

The stillness gives out. I feel nothing. I feel nothing.

What have you done? I think, as I look up at him. *What have you done?*

₿RYNN

"Brynn?" Mr. Foster leans around Charley to look at me and I stare at my boring old sneakers. "Are you doing okay over there?"

We are supposed to trust nice people. Mr. Foster is nice. He wears a stupid tie with books on it. He is the biggest nerd I've ever met. The two Mr. Fosters don't line up.

I can't stop shaking.

"I told you. She's sick," Charley says. There's something different in her voice. I don't know if she's nervous or angry or afraid.

"Are you turning into one of those *don't talk to me when we're at school* people?"

"She fainted in chorus. I want to get her to the office fast. That's all."

"Oh, Brynn," Mr. Foster says.

I don't like the sound of my name in his mouth.

"Is it your mom's test? You must feel very nervous about it. Charley says it's coming up this weekend."

I don't like the sound of my mom's name in his mouth.

"We'll talk later, Dad." Charley pulls me and we continue walking toward the office. We pass the willows. They seem to droop so low that they scratch the ground.

"I'll take her," Mr. Foster's voice calls out behind us. "No need for both of you to miss class."

"We're not doing anything in chorus. Mrs. Miller isn't even there," Charley says.

"Charlotte, I said that I'll take her."

Charley lets go of me and slinks over to the window. Mr. Foster picks up my backpack and takes my arm in his.

I'm going to die.

Mr. Foster and I walk through the glass double doors of the office. Charley is way back there with her body pressed against the windows. The willows are on the wrong side of the glass. They're just out of reach.

Mr. Foster's fingers wrap around my arm. And I see it. Suddenly, I see it in a flash. The green ink on my paper. My zipper. His fingers. And now it's dirty, wrong, shameful, a sin, his hand on mine. It happened. My body knows that it did. My mind may have been on the ceiling, but my body remembers.

I'm sorry, God. I'm so, so, sorry for the crystals and the candles and the feathers. I'm sorry for lying to Charley and Joss about being an empath. I'm sorry for being so anxious all the time and for copying my paper. If you make him let go, I'll give it all up. The rituals, the Ravens, everything. Just make him let go of my arm.

But the prayer doesn't work. Either God is too mad at me to listen, or He's not really up there. Mr. Foster knocks twice on Principal Suarez's door and then pushes it open. He still has my elbow as we step inside.

I've never been to the principal's office. It's smaller than I imagined and completely bare. It's a cold white, like the walls of a hospital.

"She fainted in chorus. I thought she could sit in here where it's quiet until someone can come pick her up."

"Oh, sweetheart. Sit down." Ms. Suarez is not usually the *sweetheart saying* type. She is usually all business and very formal. She wears suit skirts and a bun and glasses that come on and off, on and off her head. "What's your name?"

"This is Brynn McLaughlin," Mr. Foster says. He still holds my arm, even though I'm now sitting in a chair.

Get off of me. I want to scream.

Ms. Suarez is right here. She's so close. Maybe she'll help me.

I stare into her eyes. I try to make her see. I try to make her understand. But I'm no empath. I'm no psychic. I'm just Brynn. Plain old Brynn with boring clothes and a quiet voice that shakes when I get nervous.

"Oh, yes, hi Brynn," Ms. Suarez says. She gives Mr. Foster a look that says, *oh, this poor girl,* but it's not for the right reason. It's not because a monster is touching my skin. "How's mom?"

My mouth wants to say something. Anything, even just *good, fine,* would work, but nothing comes out. I'm an ice statue, carved into the chair. Mr. Foster's hand is on my arm for all of eternity. Forever and ever. Amen.

"I'll have the nurse come in and make sure you're okay and have the front desk call home. Should we call your dad? Is Mom…?"

"She's fine," I manage. "Not sick."

And I hope that's still true. I hope Mr. Foster's hands are punishment enough.

"We all care about you here." Ms. Suarez smiles down at me.

"That's true!" Mr. Foster echoes. "Absolutely."

It's like they're laughing at me.

Help, I think. *Please help.*

"Are you okay to be alone for a minute?"

I make myself nod and then they're gone, back into the hall and talking about me, talking about Mommy, getting the nurse, calling home.

I don't feel right. Like my insides have gotten too small for my body. Like I'm shrinking. I'm stuck. I'm just stuck. My silence fills the room. My silence has never been louder.

ᴊOSS

I kick the pentagram away from Foster's classroom door with the side of my sneaker. Mei's right. Charley's doing rituals without us. But if she thinks some spell is going to stop me, she's dead wrong.

Foster's door is wide open, but the lights are dim and the shades pulled down. For a second, I think I've missed him, but no, there he is, plain as day, sitting at an empty student's desk. The smart board is on but muted. Classic old man move. Subtitles and no sound.

Mr. Foster holds the remote in one hand and scribbles notes with the other. He has reading glasses on top of his head and wears his stupid book tie over a green button-down shirt.

He looks so innocent.

What if Charley's been right all along?

Maybe he's just a regular man. Maybe he's just a boring as hell, old as time English teacher. My friend Charley's dad, doing ordinary prep work for his classes. I almost turn around to leave. But I only have a split second to decide and my body moves without me. Because handsome or not and nerdy or not and nice or not, Brynn told me something. She told me something about him and I believe her.

"Mr. Foster?"

He jumps.

I shut the door. Just me and him. Him and me.

"Sorry," he gestures at the screen. He's watching the film version of *Macbeth* that my English teacher already showed my class last week. "I was very focused. Come in, Jocelyn. How can I help you?"

"Charley says you do SAT tutoring."

"Maybe you can help Charley with the math and she can help you with the English."

"I want a teacher to help me. I'm trying to get into MIT. For engineering. I need to get the English way up."

"What kind of engineering?"

"Aerospace."

"Wow! That's very specific."

I'm sweating. The school has almost no heat, but there's still disgusting sweat dripping down my face and onto my neck.

"So, do you do private tutoring?"

My voice is clear and confident, despite all the sweat.

"Alright, then, Jocelyn. There's a specific prep book that I'd like you to —"

"Oh, yeah? Which one is that?"

I take out my phone and pretend to open a browser to look for the book. Switch on my video camera instead. Draw closer to him. Shaking.

Touch me. You go ahead and touch me, you sicko.

"I like the official SAT —"

"Thank you, Mr. Foster." Closer. Closer. I stand right next to him. I video his hands. He looks at me. I see it in his eyes. I'm powerful. I'm a force. I'm-

The door bursts open.

"Hey, Mr. Foster!"

"Well, hello there, Khadija." Mr. Foster says. "Why aren't you at lunch? Actually, why aren't either of you at lunch?"

"When are we getting our quizzes back?"

"I hope tomorrow."

"Did you grade mine? You said you'd do our class first this time."

He laughs. "Get to lunch. Both of you!"

"The book?" I say to Mr. Foster. "Go ahead, Khadija. I'll catch up."

"You know what? I'm sure Charley has it. You can borrow hers instead of buying one. Sound good?"

I'm at a loss for words.

"Jocelyn? Sound good?"

"Uh—yeah. Okay."

"Come on," Khadija says. She holds the door open for me.

I head to the door with Khadija. If only she hadn't chosen that exact second to bust in... but I'll just go to tutoring. Get him alone, after school, when no one will be there to interrupt.

"And Jocelyn?" Mr. Foster calls after me.

"Yeah?"

"No cell phone."

That stops me.

"But to look stuff up?"

"Ask any of my students. I mean it. It's my only rule. Got it? SAT book and no cell phone on the table. It's too distracting."

"Got it. Fine."

I dive out the door and stumble into the hall with Khadija, where we smack right into Charley. Seeing her there makes me jump out of my skin. Takes ten years off my life.

I was wrong this morning. Her face isn't white. It's grey. Deadly.

She's following me.

"What were you doing?" Charley asks me.

Khadija bends down. Looks at the pentacle I'd kicked to the side. "Oh my God," she says, touching it with her toe.

"What. Were. You. Doing?"

"I need tutoring."

"Is this yours? Charley, this is yours, isn't it?" Khadija asks. "C'mon, Joss. Get away from her."

"I'm not afraid of Charley."

"Well, fine, then. Stay with her. I don't care. I'm going to lunch."

She runs down the hall. Coward.

Charley and I are alone.

"Joss," she says. And for a second, it's Charley. Just Charley, my friend, whose face is grey because she's terrified and sad and doesn't know what to do. I feel all of that, though I don't want to. Shield up. Shield activated.

I pull her away from her dad's door and we walk together to the end of the hall. When we're far enough away, I say, "I don't want to hurt *you*. But I have to do this."

"You have to do what?"

"Stop him."

"I protected his classroom this morning. That's why Khadija —"

"I don't believe in that. Not for one second."

"A reversal spell. You wanted to stop him. You were stopped instead."

"That doesn't even like… listen. You're so smart. You've probably read more books than our entire class combined. But you're not making any sense right now."

"You think you're so… *woke*. Why? Because your parents go to gun rallies? Because your boyfriend is black? That makes you woke? That makes you right?"

"I never said —"

"But you think it. You think it all the time."

"Seriously, you're not making sense."

"I am making sense! I am! I don't want to choose," Charley leans all her weight against a locker. Her hair is filled with static. "I shouldn't have to pick between... it's not fair. And you're forcing me to pick."

I realize it quickly. All at once. Charley *knows*. "Being loyal to your dad and doing what's right are two really different things. I feel like that's like... I feel like it's obvious, honestly."

"That's easy for you to say." Charley's face is so drained I worry she's going to fall over like Brynn did this morning. "My mom's so angry all the time. Like she's *so* angry that I figured out when I was really, really little, that I shouldn't go near her. And to this day, I avoid her. But my dad? He's patient and kind and funny and really smart; my dad is the good parent."

"But Charley, he's not."

"You don't know him. You don't live with him. You don't even have him for English. I'm begging you to stay out of it. It's not your job to defend everyone in the whole world."

Of course, it's my job. *Of course,* it is.

Charley continues. "Like you're some kind of vigilante superhero who thinks your super powers come from like... your red sneakers or something."

"My sneakers?" I can't help it. I laugh in her face.

"Stop laughing! What's wrong with you?"

"I'm sorry. It's not funny. Nothing about this is funny."

"You know what I don't think is funny? When you ask me who I want to be my boyfriend or my girlfriend. You think you're so cool because you include the word *girlfriend,* but you're not as woke as you think you are. There's more than black and white. There's more than gay or straight. There's a whole gray area that you'll never understand because you don't stop and think about anything, ever. You just fly off the handle all the time. But me? I *live* there. In the gray. You see?"

I see. I feel terrible.

"I didn't know I was—like when we played Truth? I'm really sorry. I should have known better. That's not like me."

"It feels like an attack. Every single time."

"No one's attacking you."

"They put feathers in my lunch. Did you know that?"

"Feathers? Again? Seriously, that's the best they've got? Charley, I'm sorry they're doing that, but they're so dumb. Please don't let them bother you."

"You bother me. You."

"Yes, me, and my magical sneakers."

"No, not the sneakers. I don't know why I even said —"

"Charley, I'm sorry about asking you those questions. I truly am. But I'm also worried about you. And I'm really, really worried about Brynn."

"But that's exactly what — you worry about the whole world all the time. When really, if you just stopped trying to — like if just stayed out of things, I could fix this by myself. If you would just let me."

"Rituals? Prayers? Chanting? That's not — The Ravens is a really nice idea, Charley. But it's not enough."

"What are you going to do?" she says really quietly. Almost a whisper.

"Take action," I whisper back. "My plan. If you would just stop following me around, I can help Brynn. Help everyone."

"My heart," Charley says. "It hurts. It actually..." She puts her hands over her chest like she's having a heart attack. "Help-"

"I'm trying to!"

"No. Help *me*."

"Oh, Charley." I try to use a soft tone. Like Grandma's voice was before the hurricane. "Understand. Get this. There are girls in this school who are really hurting. We don't even know how many of them are out there. I won't be on the wrong side of this. I'm going to *do* something. It's in my blood. I'm sorry, but it's just who I am."

"I'm just — I'm wrecked. I feel so wrecked."

"I can see that." She's cracking my heart in half. And it's like I'm that little girl in the closet again, trying to ignore all of that feeling down in my living room. But I also know, now that I'm grown, now that I'm strong, that this is so much bigger than being sad. This is bigger than Charley and it's definitely bigger than me. This is about anger.

Fierce, bright, anger. This is about years of rage that's been at a slow simmer and that's about to explode. "And I'm really sorry."

"I thought you were my friend."

"Hey. Hey. I *am* your friend. We can still be —"

She takes her feather out. Smooths it between her index finger and thumb like the thing is a pacifier or something.

"No, we can't."

"Okay, then," I say. "That's fine, too."

I turn away. Out of the corner of my eye, I still see her shaky fingers and the black feather, but I ignore it and start walking down the hall.

"Joss!" she yells out. "Jocelyn!"

I feel her eyes on my back, but I keep going. I make myself walk very slowly, like it's the most casual thing in the world, to walk away from a friend when she's in so much pain. I will myself not to turn around.

If this is the right thing to do, why do I feel so sick?

Once I'm out of her sight, I run. I run and run, my red vigilante superhero sneakers carrying me. I don't stop until I'm in the safety of the science lab corridor. My favorite hall. I put my bag down and lean against the cool wall. Because sick over this or not, ruining Charley or not, the time for feathers is long, long past.

There's a chemistry lab going on right across the hall. Mei is in the front row with her head propped up on her elbow. Her lab manual isn't even open. I don't see Chloe and realize I haven't seen her since she left chorus this morning. But I'm going to make things right for her now. This is for Chloe and Mei and Brynn and all the girls who feel like they need to stay silent. I'll be their voice.

"Acids donate protons," Mr. Wilkins voice leaks into the hall, "while bases accept protons."

Mr. Foster doesn't know it yet, but I've started a chain reaction. My hands curl into fists. I'm a ball of fire now, scorching every single thing in my path. I don't care if I'm harsh. I don't care if I'm searing. Acids are corrosive. Acids burn.

CHARLEY

For the first time in two years, I walk home alone.

There aren't even any squirrels or birds out on the quiet Raine streets. They've flown off, found somewhere warm. Smart creatures. Wise, gentle things.

I turn onto Main, and the storefronts come into view. The balls of pine dangle from the streetlights. At night, these clusters of lights sing of snowflakes and Christmas carols and warm scarves, made with nimble fingers and love by someone's grandmother or someone's mom. But now, in broad daylight, the lights look like afterthoughts. They're just decorations that came too soon and will be left too long and that remind those moms and grand moms to plan the meals, to finish the shopping, nothing but consumerism and greed, greed, greed.

Even the wind is angry. I wrap my arms around my waist as a gust knocks off my hood. A paper cup blows across the street and gets caught in the gutter. It bobs there, trapped between the grates.

If you listen hard enough, if you watch carefully enough, the universe talks to you. There are no coincidences. There are only signs. The cup pulled; the cup is pushed, this way and that, fighting, fighting, for freedom.

Dad?

My knees give way as the cup releases from the gutter and continues getting pulled along down the street. The sidewalk is cold. The concrete is ice.

A woman walks by me, pushing a stroller. She marches right past, doesn't see, doesn't care, because *her* baby is safe and warm, wrapped in its layers and layers of pink blankets.

Dad, come back.

But suddenly there's a hand on my arm, a good, firm grip, and I'm pulled to standing.

Ava's indigo coat, not latched, blows behind her like a cape.

"Are you hurt? What are you doing sitting on the sidewalk?"

She pulls me in close and even though she's not my mom, even though she's never knit me a scarf, I let her. She holds me and she holds me and the wind can't touch us now, the wind can't get us now. Her hug is better than the birds; it's bigger than the moon.

. . .

Ava shuts the break room door and hands me a cup of hot chocolate from the café across the street. Small marshmallows bob to the top and kiss the chocolate with sugar.

"You're shaking." She sits down in a folding chair and puts her hand on my arm. She wears rings on almost every finger: tiny crystals, silvers twisted into knots. "Is it about your dad?"

"If I tell you something, are you going to feel like you have to do something about it?"

Ava sighs in the same way that Saturn must when it settles, a song of stars and ice.

"There are lots of things that I *should* be doing, right?"

"I'm not sure what you —"

"My friend takes pain medication. Serially just takes so many pills that every day, I expect that phone call. Every day, I'm braced for it. I should intervene. I should get her into treatment, but I don't, my other friends don't. We skate past it. We ignore it, because our own lives are difficult enough. It's sick, isn't it?" She pulls her hand away from mine. "Don't grow up. I'm warning you. You think that you'll be more equipped as an adult, but… the secret is... you won't be. We're all just pretending to be competent."

"So, I *can* tell you? And you won't —"

"There's nothing you can tell me about your dad that I don't already know."

I give Ava a minute to go on, because I can tell that she has more to say that I desperately want to hear. That sadness that I often feel when we're together builds and I want to give her space to talk about it. It shouldn't always be *me, me, me*, but she doesn't continue.

"Are *you* okay? I don't feel you're really okay."

"Please, sweetheart. Don't do that. Let me take care of me."

"I just *feel* it. Your pain."

"Maybe you're feeling your own pain."

And that's a stab, right there. A knife inserted and then twisted, for good measure.

"I just," Ava continues, "I just need you to know that my heart is breaking in half for *you*. Do you understand what I'm saying? The pain that you're feeling? That's your pain, radiating right back at you."

My Ava. My compass. My only real friend.

"Well," I begin slowly. A toe in the water. "It's not just Mei and Chloe." My voice breaks, but I take a deep breath to get it back to steady. I don't want to cry.

"No, love, I'm sure that it's not."

"I saw my friend Brynn with him today. And something is wrong. I know it."

"Charley... has he ever hurt *you*?"

"Oh, God, no. Of course not! He's—that's the thing, you see? There haven't been any signs. None. And the universe always gives signs! If he did this thing, wouldn't I know?"

"But you do know," Ava says.

I see the dead bird in the grass, his hand in mine, the lightning bug that circles the tree. The slammed porch door reverberates; Mom's anger spills into the moonlight. His hand is soft, his hand is good, though the moon tugs for him. The moon begs for him. But I hold on and I hold on.

"I love him." I wrap my arms around my chest because if I don't, my grief will pour out of me and I know I don't have a stopper. "That's what no one understands."

"How can I help? What do you need?"

"Is there a spell? Or a prayer? Something that will make him stop this. I've been trying, but I don't know if it's working."

"Oh, Charley. I don't—I'm not sure that it works that way."

"Please, Ava. You must know of some ritual. Maybe there are special crystals. Something more advanced!" I take my phone out of my pocket. It will be easy enough to look up online, but Ava takes the phone right out of my hands and puts it upside down on the table.

"We can pray for your inner strength. We can focus our intentions on your resolve. But we can't influence someone else's choices. I don't believe in that."

"But is it *possible?*"

Ava doesn't answer me. No one answers me when it actually matters.

"Something must have—something had to have happened to him, right? Otherwise, why would he...? Why would anyone? So, if we could find a spell to make him see —"

"There's no spell, love."

"That you *know* of. Ask your friends. There must be some kind of possession spell. I can embody him, so he'll stop."

"You're talking about black magic."

"But for a really good purpose! So, we'll just talk to your friends and see."

"Will you talk to your *mom*?" Ava interrupts me.

"I didn't know you were a comedian."

"If you won't talk to her, I feel like I'm going to need to instead."

"You just promised me you wouldn't!"

"Someone has to, Charley." Her voice breaks.

"Ava, what's the *matter?*"

Ava, even my Ava, thinks I'm too young or too stupid to understand her problems. She'd rather talk to an adult than to me. It's cruelly, maliciously unfair, to be granted these powers — these sweeping, overwhelming feelings of knowing—and then to not be taken seriously. To be treated like a stupid child. A stupid little girl.

"Listen, sweetie. There's a time for magic and a time for prayer and a time to let the universe run its course. And then there are other times, like now, that demand action. I want you..." Ava looks up at the ceiling. There are tears in her eyes. I hate it when adults cry. I've seen so much anger, and I've seen so much ignorance, but a grownup's crying fills me. It hurts.

"What?" I whisper. "Ava, what is it?"

"I want you to be stronger than I was at your age. I want you to use your voice and demand justice. Otherwise, you'll regret it for the rest of your life. I can tell you this with certainty. But if you don't, or won't, or can't—then I will."

"You sound just like Joss. She has some kind of plan. I don't even know what —"

"Then let her help you. Let me help you. You're not alone."

But of course, that's an outright lie. I'm being backed into corners by people who are supposed to care.

"You're threatening me."

"Threatening you? Absolutely not, Charley. I'm trying to help you."

"Then give me a spell. Just one."

"I can't do that," she says quietly.

"Then I quit," I whisper. "I'm done."

"You'll never be done. You're so much stronger than that."

"I mean, I quit the bookstore. Jabberwocky."

"Charley?"

"I said I'm done."

I get up and shove the hot chocolate to the middle of the table. It tips and splashes onto my phone. Everything is destroyed. Everything is ruined.

I grab my wet phone and bag and push out of the break room door. There are a few customers pulling books off of the shelves. Ben is at the counter. I don't stop to say goodbye. The door to Jabberwocky jingles and Main Street greets me with a blast of cold. There's still no one around. The people, like the birds, are hibernating from the coming cold. The glittering pine is garish and stupid when there's no one around to see it. A single car passes through the road and then the silence returns. The world is sick with silence.

Joss

"You wanna do something?" Malik asks. He's thrown himself all over the couch in the rental house, leaving no room for me, which is totally fine, to be honest. I wedge myself onto the edge of the middle cushion with my back buried into his stomach.

"Such as?" I mean to sound flirty, but I'm pretty sure it just comes out as awkward.

"I don't know. Watch a movie?"

His voice is low and a little raspy. I've figured out that's the voice he uses after he's just talked to his dad on the phone. But obviously, I know better than to ask him about it. So even though his voice is quiet, I don't ask him what's wrong. Maybe someday, when we've been going out for much longer—a year, two years, a ring, the kids, the whole nine—then he'll tell me (in his own words — not my brother's) what makes him so sad.

"A movie? But what about calculus?"

He's still wearing glasses from studying. His final exams are coming up soon and his math textbook is open on the "coffee table." Air quotes needed because the table is actually a door that Malik and his roommate took off of an upstairs closet and balanced on top of two folding chairs. The hole where the knob used to be works like a cup-holder. They should definitely sell door-tables at Target. I'd buy one. I'd buy ten if it meant supporting Malik.

"I can't concentrate on that when there's a beautiful girl on my lap."

"I'm not on your lap." Look at me, being all cute, when inside I'm actually dying. I've never had a boyfriend before Malik. I probably *could* have. Julian used to flirt with me in freshmen homeroom, but I'd just started hanging out with Charley and she'd made these weird rules about dating, which I now understand and feel really terrible about. Need to check myself sometimes. But anyway, finally, one hot summer night, when Leo was out of the way in the kitchen at Sebastian's, Malik asked me if I wanted to hang out, *you know, without your loser brother*. And I forgot about Charley and I forgot about the feathers and the crystals and the rules, and all I saw in front of me was Malik. A path straight to him. Lit up by lightning.

"We can fix that."

He pulls me up so I'm sitting on his stomach and I can feel his abs beneath his shirt. Malik goes to the gym every day and runs every other day. He took me running once at the park and then couldn't stop laughing when I threw myself on the ground. I was nauseous and my legs were burning after jogging only like a half-mile in the blazing summer heat. I'm a sprinter, that's true enough, my red sneakers flashing. But I have trouble with distance. Can't keep up for long with a pace as fast as mine. *You. Are. Adorable,* he'd said and kissed a drop of sweat off of my forehead.

"Hey. You know what today is?" I ask.

"Monday?"

"December 9th!"

"Uh-huh?"

"And you asked me out on July 9th."

"I can't believe you remember that. You don't have a scrapbook, do you? Tell me you don't save receipts and movie tickets and stuff. Actually, tell me you *do.*"

"Don't," I say. "*But.* What I'm trying to say is that today is our six-month anniversary. And so, if you wanted... we could, maybe. Do something?" I run my fingers over his stomach and try to keep my face serious, but I almost burst out laughing.

"Are we even legal? College boy, you know."

Adorable *and* respectful. I cannot.

"The consenting age in New Jersey is sixteen. I may or may not have looked it up."

"So... want to know what I think is really sexy?"

I'm dying. I'm actually dying right now.

"What?" I say, in my regular voice, before realizing that if this was TV, I'd probably have dropped my voice very low.

"When you help me with differential equations."

I punch him lightly in the stomach.

"You know I'm going to have to take all the way up to Calculus IV for my major," I say. "Is that sexy?"

"For your major? Are you in college already?"

He rubs my back with his knuckles.

"For aerospace. If I get in, I mean."

"*When* you get in."

"About that," I say. "Do you still have your flip camera?"

"Huh?"

Nice segue, Joss.

"You mean you want to record us... 'doing calculus'?" he asks.

It takes me a minute to get that. Like, legit, it takes an entire minute. "Ew! No! I'm doing SAT tutoring. I want to film the sessions so I can review them later."

"I don't understand. You're *doing* SAT tutoring, or you're getting tutored?"

"Getting tutored."

"Your PSAT is already —"

"Do.You.Have.The.Camera?"

"Somewhere, I guess. I don't know. Thing's so old. Just use your —"

"Tutor has no chill about cell phones. Can. You. Just. Find. It?" I punctuate each word with a little kiss.

"I'll get right on it." He laughs and then pulls me off his stomach and moves over so I can lay next to him on the couch. He moves my hair and kisses the back of my neck.

"One more thing," I say.

"Zero more things."

"No, seriously. One more thing. I need it for right after school this Friday. I can't go home first. My dad doesn't even know I'm doing this."

"You're *sneaking* SAT tutoring? Bad. Ass."

"Oh, you have no idea."

"That librarian girl must be rubbing off on you."

"A) Her name is Charley and B) No. This is all me."

His knuckles return to my back and make me want to stop everything. Just: Pause.

"In all seriousness, you'll get into MIT without the extra tutoring, you know."

"You have no idea how competitive the program is. And the only other place I'd even consider is Georgia Tech, which is also really hard to get into."

"What about our good old county college?"

"Would I get to stay here with you?"

I'd meant my question to be cute, but Malik looks at me like there's a rainstorm coming in. He doesn't like to talk about the future. I'd already learned that lesson when I'd asked him about the mirror.

"So, why aerospace engineering?" he finally asks. "You want to fly?"

"Oh, no, Malik," I say, tracing my fingers on his arm. "I'm going to —"

"Send men into space?"

He lifts his head up and kisses my ear and my cheek. His warm hands burrow beneath my sweater. The couch disappears. The table-door vanishes. I see the planets. I see the stars.

CHARLEY

There's nothing in *iWitchcraft* about doing spells to control someone else's actions. Just like Ava had said, it's this sort of weird area among witches. Some think it's fine if it's for a good reason and others think it's morally wrong to do a spell on someone else. I don't get it. The universe is painted in shades of colors that are too hard to name — the raw edge of the shore on the sand, its raging foam, the sky, its reflection sometimes blue, sometimes pink, with its sunsets that pop and burst, draping the morning in the colors I love so much.

Since *iWitchcraft* and Ava won't help me, I'm finding everything I need on the internet, posted by fellow bloggers. I haven't hidden under my blankets like this since I was a little kid, reading with a flashlight after Dad had told me to turn off the light and go to sleep.

I create a new post and save it as a draft. I never hit publish until I actually test my spells. I try to do my part in making the internet a reliable place for information, unlike what Dad says about not using it for research papers.

Banishing Spell Notes:

The spell can be black magic or white magic depending on the witch's intention.

Goal: Person's energy will not harm anyone anymore, and instead, will be re-directed right back (similar to reversal spell I did at school).

Question: Can I achieve the not harming anyone without having the negative energy reflected on Dad?

Materials Needed: Parchment paper, sea salt, an object belonging to or photograph of the person's energy you are trying to banish

Use carefully, and only in times of extreme importance, because there can be danger in trying to control someone's free will.

Whatever is sent out into the universe will come back to me three-fold.

There's a knock on the door, and I throw my blankets off. Mom comes in without waiting for me to give her the okay. She's still wearing scrubs.

"Were you sleeping?"

"A little nap."

"There's nothing in the house to eat, so we thought we'd go to out for dinner."

"On a Monday?"

"What's wrong with Monday?"

"Nothing. We just never. And I have so much homework."

"You have to eat anyway, right?"

She's trying to be friendly. But just underneath her words, which sound fine enough, is this not-so-hidden fury that threatens to pour out of her at any given moment. I sit up in bed. Blink. Try to come back to this world, the one with moms and dinner invitations, when really, my foot is still in that other place, with the crystals, the salt, the sage. It's getting harder and harder to switch back and forth so quickly.

"But going out to eat takes longer than eating at home."

"Charley, please. For the love of God, just put some shoes on. Where do you want to go? Stay in Raine, or — maybe you want to go to that place Jocelyn's always talking about?"

"*Sebastian's?* Absolutely not. You'll hate it."

"Okaaaaaay," Mom says. "We'll stay in Raine, then. Shoes, coat, please."

"You always talk to me the way parents talk to their little kids at the store." Of course, as of this afternoon, I no longer work at the store, but I decide not to mention this tiny detail. "I'm not a baby."

"I'm sorry."

"Okay."

"Okay?"

"I said okay."

"We'll see you downstairs, then."

She shuts my door.

I roll off of my mattress, put my tablet inside of my engraved box, close the lid, and shove it far beneath my bed. Though, even tucked away, the draft calls out to me. The spell waits.

·　　·　　·

We settle on the brick oven pizza place diagonally across from Jabberwocky. Mom insists on a window seat, so looking across the street, I catch glances of Ava straightening books and scurrying around the store.

Mom pulls a bottle of wine out of her purse.

"Classy."

"It's BYOB!"

Mom was born and raised in New York City, where, I guess, there's no such thing as restaurants that let you bring your own wine. Even though Mom's now lived in New Jersey longer than I've even been alive, she still seems to get a little thrill about lugging bottles of wine around in her bag. If she wasn't so angry all the time, I might think it was cute.

We watch out the window a little. Ava's head bobs in and out of view.

"How's Ava?" Dad asks. "Still getting around via broom stick?"

"So disrespectful, Dad."

"Maybe I should bring her in to talk with my classes about the witches in *Macbeth*."

"Those are just rumors, no? Wasn't she an actor?" Mom asks.

"She *is* an actor. Why can't she be a witch and an actor at the same time?"

"You are suddenly very defensive of witches," Dad says.

"The witches in *Macbeth* are total caricatures. Real witches act nothing like that."

"And how would you know that, little Bronte?"

"Please don't call me that anymore."

Mom hands the wine bottle to our server and gestures that she needs a corkscrew. "Quickly, please. I never have a clue what these two are talking about."

"Anyway," Dad continues, "Even if Billy Shakes was really off on the witchcraft stuff, the weird sisters are still very powerful, no? Didn't Miss Carter talk to you guys about feminism in *Macbeth*? I always tell my classes that —"

"The witches have beards, Dad. Who even knows if they're actually women?"

"Purposefully androgynous —"

"Okay, but why? Because women can't be powerful in and of themselves? They need to have masculine traits?"

"Symbolism. Switched gender roles. The beards show how much influence the weird sisters have over the male-dominated landscape of the play."

"Women don't need beards to have influence."

Nothing, even book chats with Dad, will ever be the same. Everything means something else. It's like real life has become a book and the things around me are symbolic. The wine stands for delusion. It represents all that I have pretended that I don't know about Dad. The windows—clarity, a sense of finally seeing rightly. And Dad, talking about feminism and gender roles? It's not just irony. It's deeper than that. Juxtaposition, maybe, but there needs to be a stronger word. A darker word.

"Women need to support each other," I say.

"What does that have to do with what we're talking about?"

"Not beards, not… the only thing women need is the support of other *women*."

"I don't know if that's the *only* thing women need."

"And what, may I ask, do you know about what women need?" Mom interjects. She smiles at me. This is a switch.

The server comes to take our order. We haven't even glanced at the menus, but Dad tells him we'll take a pizza with mushrooms. I don't want mushrooms.

"Someday," I say, my teeth grit, "Women are going to take over the world. It's going to be shaken up like a snow globe. And the men are going to land on the bottom, all upside down, and the women are going to be on top."

Mom is wide-eyed, her fingers around her glass. "Damn straight," she laughs.

"Where is this coming from?" Dad asks. "From *Macbeth*?"

"Joss, Brynn and I — we used to talk about this all the time." This is sweet Charley on fire. This is dear, adorable, empathetic Charley, turned warrior, like Joss. "Do you even think about that? About how you, as a white man, have every door open for you. And how mom and I, as women, aren't granted the same privileges that you are. And how marginalized women — like Ava — like Mei — have to jump over even more hurdles than I do, just because I'm white."

"Are you angry with me about something?" Dad asks.

The room turns red.

It's like the bowling alley all over again. Power tingles at my fingertips. I feel like maybe, just maybe, I could will his water glass to shatter by mere intention. And suddenly there are two roads in front of me. I can see them up ahead like in that Robert Frost poem. Black and white. Plain and simple. Just like Joss sees the world. Down the first path, I say, *no, not angry, just a discussion* and we go back to pretending everything's fine and I let my grief take over and I let my love for him take over and I backtrack, blame my words on reading too much Jane Austen, blame it on the Bronte trio, on *Macbeth*. Or, I could take the second path, the "road not taken," and say, *I know what you've done.*

But there are only seconds to respond. And so, I relax the energy sparking in my hands and avoid his question completely. I say, instead, "I'm going to fix the gender gap. The divide."

"That's a really noble idea. But—how?" Dad asks, as the server comes back and places a stand with our pizza on the middle of the table.

How?

How.

It's exactly what Joss had asked me in the locker room on Thursday, when I'd given the girls their gifts. I'm so sick of that question. I'm so tired of everyone having to be so literal all the time, when anyone can see the world is full of symbols. The universe will take care of me. The energy will guide me.

"Because you're talking a great game —"

"Oh, leave her alone, Declan. She's exploring new ideas. It's a good thing," Mom interrupts.

"It's my teacher's blood. Can't help it. It's my job to get her to think more critically."

"She's not your student."

"Thank God," I mumble. I shove my plate to the other side of the table.

"I thought you always wanted to be in my class! And what's the matter? You're not eating?"

"Didn't want mushrooms."

"Pick them off?"

I stare at him a long minute.

"Recognition," I say. "That's how."

"Recognition of what?"

But I refuse to say anything else.

I watch them eat their pizza in silence. Every once in a while, Mom looks up at me like she wants to say something, but she stays quiet. For the first time in a long time, I don't feel her anger pouring into me. I feel something else, something softer, a feeling without a name.

Maybe there's a third road that Frost never mentions in his poem — a path made from trees that I knocked down myself. Black and white, good and evil, Brynn and Dad. I choose it all. I choose not to choose. I won't take the road less traveled; I'll take the road never traveled — until now.

I settle back into my chair and look out onto Main Street. It gets dark so early in the late fall. Out on the street, the wind rocks the balls of pine back and forth. A woman buttons her coat. The white lights shine.

•   •   •

The night is dead dark.

Mom's asleep in their bedroom at the end of the hall, and Dad's snoring on the couch in the living room. I don't remember when they stopped sleeping in the same bed, but even when Mom's on shift, Dad chooses the couch, like even Mom's empty pillows and the lingering scent of NICU baby powder and creams on the sheets are too much of a reminder of her.

Though my parents' sounds are quiet, their presences are large. We're pulled together by a kind of glowing string, each one of us the points on a gleaming triangle. The life-force that I've felt around me since I was a child has been getting stronger. I feel it everywhere. I feel it all the time.

I click on my purple bulb and shadows creep over the rug. I quietly sweep the room with my broom to get rid of any bad energy and then bury it back in the closet, hidden behind my sweaters and jackets and everyday things. I shut the door and try to pretend those clothes aren't in there. They don't feel like me. Or, they don't feel like me right now.

I too, like Dad, lead a double life. I'm never fully one, never fully the other, just always both, or always none, floating, alone, alone, until Joss and Brynn and Mei and Chloe came along, two years ago now, and said, *yes, Charley, we hear the moon, too. Yes, Charley, we also feel the vibrations.*

But somehow, I'm alone again and crying while I create a circle around me with black salt. I close the circle off and sit down beside my small altar: Dad's book-tie, a black candle, some sage, Mom's calligraphy pen, and some drawing paper. I light the candle and the flame is small, but steady. I put a match to the sage and hold the little bundle by the tip as the ashes fall into the bowl. I don't speak, but take slow breaths in to calm down. On the inhale, I meditate: *With the power of air, I purify this circle.*

I uncap the pen and scratch it against the paper. My handwriting is wild. I will never have Mom's steady, artistic hand. My art is that of the wind. The sky.

Declan Foster.

I fold Dad's name in half and then half again and place the paper on top of his tie. I twist the tie into a knot around the paper to hold it in place. My fingers don't shake.

"Your hands and wicked heart will not hurt anyone anymore," I whisper. I'm supposed to add something about *because your energy will come back to you instead*, like I'd done with my reversal spell on Joss, but I can't do that to him. After all, this is the third road. The road never traveled. "I banish your negative spirit from our school."

I create a second knot and then a third, repeating the same words. "I banish your wicked heart, Dad. You cannot harm anyone from this moment forward."

The house is quiet. The energetic triangle glitters, connects us while my parents sleep. I'm at the top point of that triangle now. I feel perfectly, absolutely still.

"Air, Wind, Fire, Earth: Stay if you will, but leave if you must."

I blow out the candle and wait for the sage to burn out. Then I pick up Dad's tie, knotted around the paper, and creep into the hall. I have to bury it.

I sneak down the stairs with the light of my phone and come to a dead stop when I get to the living room, where Dad continues snoring. I tiptoe past him and head to the kitchen, which has a side-door that leads to our garage. I rummage through Mom's gardening tools until I find a small trowel and head out into the cold night.

Once outside, I dig the trowel deep into the earth, which is nearly frozen, the consistency of crumbling rock. Outside like this, beneath the dying moon, the universe whispers to me. There's a lonely wail, an icy gust meant for me alone. For me — alone.

Careful, Charley. Beware, Charley.

I put down the shovel and look out into the sky. The moon is waning, its light slivered and crisp. The nights are blacker than they used to be; the moon quieted by the turning shadow of the earth. I let the shadows overtake me. I stand out there in the dark.

฿RYNN

"You can't bury yourself like this," Mommy says.

She opens up my blinds and ties back the curtains, and the Tuesday morning light pours into my room. I've had the same lavender drapes and the same white dresser and the same giant stack of construction paper, which is now cursed, since I was a little girl. I usually love all the sun that gets into my room. I like being able to say, *and that's where Cousin Talia threw up her hot dog,* or *do you remember the M&M that got stuck in the rug*? The memories pile until my room overflows with them. But this morning, the light hurts my eyes. The lit-up memories make me tired.

"Brynn," Daddy says. I feel the indent of him as he sits by my feet and tugs the blanket off of my head. "You have to go to school."

I'm never going to go to school ever, ever again. Call in the home school teacher, call in the tutor, pull up the online classes. There will be no fainting, no chorus, no plagiarized papers, and definitely, without a doubt, no Mr. Foster for forever and ever. Amen. And there I go again. The joke's on me. I can't escape Catholicism no matter how hard I try.

"We know you're embarrassed about fainting but the more you don't do something that you're afraid to do, the more it forms a groove in your brain that prevents you from doing it even further."

"Not your client, Daddy."

He tries to therapy me *all the time*. When I was little, he thought he could talk away my nervousness… but all that talking? It only made me more anxious and so it was like this never-ending circle of me being nervous, of Daddy getting me to talk about it, and then me getting anxious talking about my anxiety.

"Dr. E. said you're fine to go back to school," Mommy says.

Dr. E, Mommy says, like I'm five-years-old and can't pronounce his full name. Our urgent care visit after school yesterday is one reason I can't leave the house ever again. *Deep breath*, Dr. E. had said. The stethoscope was cold, and I gasped as his fingers accidentally brushed against my skin. I opened my mouth to speak. *Stop*, I'd try to say, but no sound came out. It's like I was screaming silently in a dream and couldn't wake myself up. The fluorescent lights were bright and hot over my head and Dr. E. put his hand on my shoulder to steady me as he moved the stethoscope to my back. *Breathe deeply, please,* he said again. He touched the metal to my back and touched it to my back, and I was stuck there. I was trapped in Foster's classroom again. The green ink—*Plagiarism, See Me*—stared out at me. Mr. Foster's fingers crawled around to my waist. They moved to my zipper.

"Take half your pill, sweetheart, and then you're going to have to get dressed and get to school," Mommy continues.

"Even half a pill and I'm basically unconscious. I can't take one before school. We've talked about this sixty-five million times."

What I don't tell them is that the pills are under my pillow. That I feel safer with them there.

"We'll all feel better after my mammogram. But we can't hide out until then. Have to live our lives."

"That's not why."

Oh Lordy, Lordy. I'm going to cry. Does anyone cry more than me? Is there a single person on this earth who could possibly compete? If there was a tear-measuring competition in the Olympics, I'd be chomping my teeth down on a gold medal. I'd take it, hands down.

"If it's not the scan," Mommy says, "Then what? Did something happen?"

There are these words. There are all of these words that I can't say that get all stuck in my throat and come out like: *asdtflj;iobvkiereasdf!* like a baby hit random keys on a keyboard except the keyboard is my mouth and my brain, which are all scrambled up, lightning flashing, circuits burning, fried.

I want to tell them. I'm not one of those teenagers who wears black and is mad all the time and gets secret tattoos and wants to run away with her friends because she thinks her parents are stupid or wrong or don't understand her. I love my parents. I love my room. I love the red stain on my rug from the M&M, and sometimes, I just want to stay little and little and little and I want to cry out, *fix it, Mommy, kiss my knee Mommy*, but the problem is: sometimes your mommy gets breast cancer, and she needs you to kiss her instead. And sometimes… it's twisted around more than that and adults, who are supposed to protect their kids… teachers —

"It's like there's this wall," I finally say. "And I'm on one side of it, while Charley and Joss are on the other side. I'm just different."

"Generalized anxiety disorder…"

Generalized anxiety disorder is the wrong name. My anxiety is not general. It's *so* not general. It's actually really specific. That's what gets me so mad. I get nervous about such very, very clear things. When I was younger, I would get scared that Mommy forgot to sign my homework and that my teacher wouldn't take it. I checked it over and over and over. Five times in the car. Six times when I was already at school. I snuck the homework out of my folder like a kid trying to hide candy during class.

Did she sign it? Yes, she did. And the anxiety only got bigger from there, when there were actual things to be anxious about, like *did the cancer spread to far away lymph nodes or just the close ones.*

"...can lead to feelings of deep depersonalization."

And now, I'm anxious that if I go back to school, Mr. Foster will get to me again. But if I tell my parents about this, they'll snap. Attack. Alligators after a fish. And then what? Charley. Charley who loves me. Charley who sees me. Charley whose life will be unwound like string.

I don't have generalized anxiety disorder. I have specific anxiety disorder. If I made that illness up, they should call me in so that I can write about it for their textbooks. They should put it in Daddy's DSM book, which is this huge thing, Bible thick, that's really just lists of codes that tell him what might be wrong with people so their insurance will pay for treatment. It's all a scam. It's all a joke. There's no code for what I have.

"Please, just listen to me. Just really listen to me. I never stay home from school. Never been in trouble. There are people at school who are doing drugs, sneaking out. I don't do any of those things. Just...please. I can't go to school today. I won't go."

My parents give each other a look. They say fifty silent things to each other and I know that I've won.

"Just for today," Mommy finally says. "Do you understand? This can't go beyond today."

One day at a time. That's fine. For today, I'll be safe and warm and tucked away at home. Willow will sleep next to my hip.

"But you'll be here alone. Daddy and I can't miss work."

"I never asked you to miss —"

"I know you didn't."

Mommy leans down to kiss my forehead. Daddy gives my foot a squeeze.

"I've been praying for you. I prayed the rosary the entire time I was driving to pick you up when you were sick at school. And even in the waiting room at the urgent care. You're always in my mind and heart. You know that, right?"

The rosary? Prayers won't help me. Not when God points His angry finger straight down through the clouds directly at me. *Witch*, He says. *Heretic*.

"Close, please," I point to the curtains.

They flip the blinds back down, click off my light, and shut the door. Willow's not here. Got locked out into a different part of the house. Maybe he's by the food dish with the fish bone print or on the thick blue blanket on the window seat we put out just for him. Wherever he is, even though it's not with me, he's peaceful. He's still. The quiet returns. I sink into it. I slide into the dark.

• • •

I dream of witches.

Charley, Joss, and a masked girl dance around a bonfire. The flames glow bright against the winter water. The girls are barefoot and shouting. They want the masked girl to show her face. And suddenly, instead of watching the scene from the side, I *am* that masked girl. I don't want to uncover my face, but Charley and Joss sprinkle colored powder over the kindling, and the fire cracks and leaps, and my hands are pulled by an invisible force. I rip the mask off and uncover my bald head. The other girls back away from me. They turn and run toward the tide and dive into the icy water like seeing my face scarred their skin, and the water is the antidote. I throw the mask into the fire and watch it burn.

There's a ringing sound. A *ding, ding* that calls me back from the ocean. My eyes fling open, and I say hello to the lavender and white of my bedroom. The blinds are still closed, but the light comes in. I reach for my phone. Four o'clock. I slept for the entire school day.

The doorbell rings.

My phone vibrates in my hand.

Are you home? Can you let me in?

A text message from Charley.

I leap out of bed and run down the stairs. I'm wearing mismatched pajamas: red flannel bottoms with a long-sleeved Cookie Monster shirt. Mental Note: Burn these pajamas.

I pull open the front door.

Charley looks different.

Her red hair is loose underneath a black knit hat. She steps into the house and shrugs out of her coat, which she throws over a chair in the living room. She wears a draped black sweater that comes to her knees over dark tights and boots. Her socks are grey. Boring, like mine. She looks older. Sadder. Even more pale than usual. She looks like the Charley from my dream.

"Did you go to the doctor?" She plops down on our couch. Whenever my parents aren't home, she acts like my house is her house. Imagine if we were sisters? I think my life would be completely different if I had a sister. "Did they figure out why you fainted yesterday?"

And though her clothes are dark, and her face is gray, her voice is still dazzling. I think of her as a rainbow bursting between clouds. Her words are colored and large and they make people turn around to look. She was teased a lot because she doesn't know how to blend in. But with a voice like that and with thoughts so bright, why should she try?

"Were you anxious about the mammogram, or what? Because that's going to be fine, you know. I brought some quartz. I thought if you wanted, we could do a healing ritual without Joss being all negative. We could sneak one in before your parents get home."

She's talking very, very fast. She does this sometimes, so it's not that weird, but this is fast even for her.

"I mean, we'll probably have to do it once every six months or so from now on."

She blabbers on about my mom and quartz and rituals for a bit. I let her. But I know why she really came over. She knows why she really came over.

I'm tired of lying. Of feeling like I'm underwater and everyone else is above me in the air. I can see the shapes of people up there above me, but they're fuzzy and weird. Glowing blobs in the sun. Fractured in the waves.

"I'm really grateful," I finally break in. "You know I am."

"I can barely hear you."

I take a huge gulp of air and try to calm my anxiety. I look for Willow, but the doorbell must have scared him. He's nowhere in sight. "I think that whatever you did —*we* did — worked to heal Mommy. And I can never thank you enough for that."

"Along with the surgery and chemo, of course —"

"But Charley?" I say her name as loudly as I can manage and sit next to her on the couch. "I don't think that's why I fainted."

"What are you trying to say? Can you please just say it? Please."

"I can't," I whisper. "It's like my mouth won't let me."

"I *feel*... I just. I felt it yesterday when we ran into my dad in the hallway."

"Felt what?"

She's quiet for a long time and looks down at her lap.

"Charley, felt what?" I ask again.

She snaps her head up again and looks right at me, like she'd decided about something. "Why did you tell me you made the whole thing up?"

"Oh," I say. It's all I can say.

I wish the cushions would turn into quicksand so I'd sink into the couch and disappear forever.

"Oh," I say again, because I'm still like that baby tapping away at the computer. I'm coming up with nothing but jumbled letters and random exclamation points. My thoughts don't make sense. My words won't come out. *Pop. Boom.* The circuits explode and then: nothing. I'm on the wrong side of the water again. Nothing looks real. Charley is far away.

"I guess I know why," Charley continues. Her voice is muffled. "I basically gave you no choice. I was such an awful friend. Such a bad person."

"No," I whisper. "Terrible situation. Not—bad person."

"I wanted to tell you I think I've fixed it now. He won't hurt you or anybody else ever again."

"Police? Did you…?"

"No, no, no. I did a banishing spell. It'll prevent him from harming anyone else. I feel like it's… I just think it's going to work."

I stand up from the couch so fast, my foot catches on the coffee table.

"It's not really black magic. I read all about it. It just depends on intention and my intention is good. I did it to protect you."

You did it to protect yourself, I think. I've never been angry with Charley before. Or, I've never let myself be angry with her. But these are just more words that I can't say out loud. There are so many of them piled up in me that one day, I'm going to explode.

"I don't feel so good," I whisper. "Can you— maybe—like come back another time?"

"Oh," Charley says. I guess both of us are just going to say 'oh' to each other all afternoon. She looks surprised. "Okay… no problem."

She stands up, shifts her backpack, and heads to the front door. I open it up for and she goes outside.

"Hey, Brynn, are you… okay?"

"Tired," I say. "Just… tired."

"Okay…"

I watch her turn and walk down the stairs and cross the lawn. The wind gets inside my pajamas and I shiver. I start to close the door just as Charley turns back to wave. I see her, but shut the door anyway, before I can wave back. I don't bother opening it again. I press my palm against the wood.

CHARLEY

Brynn's not at school again. She hasn't come back since she fainted in chorus on Monday. Out yesterday, not here again today, wanted nothing to do with me when I went to visit her yesterday afternoon. But that's okay. I've been prepared for this, ready to face this day and the next and the next, alone. It's not that hard. It's not that difficult. It only takes a deep breath, a steeling of the will, clothes, black, impenetrable, my long sweater, the one that sweeps past my knees, with the hood I can pull over my face. Safe.

Mrs. Miller takes attendance. She's the only teacher that still calls our names out loud this late in the school year. It's so lazy. When I become an English professor, I'm going to learn my students' names on day one and remember them forever. That's just human decency. Just kindness.

"Charlotte Foster," Mrs. Miller says.

"*Witch*," I hear, from the top riser.

"Bruja,"

"Devil worshipper!"

"Charlotte Foster?" Mrs. Miller says again.

I can't get myself to raise my hand. Can't get myself to say 'here.'

"So what if she *is* a witch?" Joss yells out, without looking up from her music. "Seriously, so what if she is?"

"Ladies?" Mrs. Miller asks. "Everything okay?"

Oblivious. Dumb. When I'm an English professor, I'm going to pay attention. I'm going to notice the quiet ones, the girls with hoods over their heads who don't usually wear hoods over their heads. But not Mrs. Miller. Not now.

Joss stares straight ahead after her outburst, her back aligned and strong and defiant. Mei and Chloe whisper together. Khadija and Emma giggle.

I feel crumbly. I feel weak in the knees. But this is the price. This is the cost. The universe being thrown back around, three-fold. I'm one with my sisters now, generations of women burned. I straighten my back. Pull my hood tighter over my face. Let them whisper. Let them laugh. I don't care if I'm on fire.

•　　•　　•

There are feathers glued all over my locker. Primary colors. Blue, green, bright red, unnatural, gaudy, probably purchased on the internet for two dollars and delivered the very next day through some stupid skein girl's parents' account.

I wind my combination into the lock and open the door. There are more feathers inside, shoved into the tiny air ducts. They've settled onto my books, onto my lunch bag. I spin around. The skein girls are everywhere.

"They're for your collection," one girl says.

"You can always use more, right?"

They point and they laugh, their dainty little hands covering their lips, pursed and pink, shining with cupcake and cookie dough scented lip glosses. I hate them. I hate them all.

"Shut up."

"That's not very nice, Charlotte."

"I'm warning you."

"You're *warning* us?"

I raise my arms up into the air. Like I can touch the ceiling, like I can burst through it and touch the sky, beyond, beyond, the dark of deep space, the bright bursts of colored gas, the deep craters of the moon.

What's she doing?

They scatter. Stupid waddling geese.

She's such a freak!

"I curse you," I scream.

If this is what they want me to be, then this is what I'll be.

"I curse all of you!"
Get away from her!
They fumble. They trip. They run.
I lower my arms.

ᏴRYNN

Friday afternoon.

The white lights of the waiting room are so bright that they're giving me a headache. I guess it's because I haven't been outside of the house in a week. I feel a little nauseous and keep taking deep breaths so that I don't throw up all over the clinic's floor. Not the best way to spend a Friday morning. Not the first place I want to be for my first venture out into the world.

Mommy and Daddy and I have been sitting around in the clinic's waiting room for an hour already. The radiologist is looking at the results of the scan and will call Mommy in soon. This place is all the way in Warden instead of the one right in Raine, but Mommy's oncologist had suggested it because the radiologist is on site and gives results right away. Most places don't. And we've been down that road before. The waiting will kill you quick as poison.

It's just the three of us in the waiting room and one other lady who came alone. She's youngish. Maybe thirty. She sits close to the window and stares out of it, the way Joss's grandma does. She's not here for a routine test. If you come here often enough like we do, you can always tell.

I don't feel good.

"Are you okay?" Mommy asks.

I turn to look at her but see she's talking to the lady, not to me.

That's fine.

Unlike Joss's grandma, the lady turns from the window to look at us.

"First mammogram after lumpectomy," she says.

"Oh, yes, I remember that one," Mommy answers. She once told me that the good thing about cancer is the way it opened her up to strangers. *I'm going to become an ambassador,* she told me. *From here on out, I'm going to scoop people up and hold their pain the best I can.*

"The surgery sometimes changes the breast tissue. So even if they say something is abnormal, it doesn't mean that it's something bad. It means they need to establish a new baseline for what's normal for you."

We know all about that.

The first time Mommy went for a scan after surgery and chemo were finished was one of the most terrifying days of my life. I took a whole pill almost every day that week and over dinner made a terrible mistake. I'd been reading online about breast cancer for weeks and really thought Mommy should have done a mastectomy rather than a lumpectomy. Actually, I thought she should have done a double mastectomy. Just lob both of them off and never have to worry about a mammogram ever again. It's not that cancer can't come back after a mastectomy, but the chances are lower and the doctor can just do a physical exam instead of these scans every six months to a year.

Don't you love me and Daddy enough to get a mastectomy? I had whispered at dinner. The pill made me so tired I could barely keep my head up. She looked at me for a long time and then got up from the table. That wrecked me more than if she had yelled at me.

Charley had said it didn't matter that Mommy didn't get a mastectomy. Mastectomy or lumpectomy, radiation or chemo, it didn't matter. The Ravens would keep her safe. And you know what? We *did.*

I feel around for the feather in my coat pocket. It's still there, right next to the bottle of pills that I'd tucked in there late last night. The rituals helped Mommy before and hopefully they will help her again, as long as God isn't trying to punish me for messing around with that stuff. *Let Mr. Foster's hands be punishment enough.* This has been my silent thought all morning.

"Thank you," the lady says to Mommy. "It helps to talk about it. My husband never wants to talk about it."

"Your family is scared, too. It's a family disease," Mommy says and looks at me.

I wonder if she thinks about that night at dinner as much as I do. I'm so stupid. I'm such an idiot. I don't know if I'll ever have the courage to say sorry for that or if it will become one of those things that I whisper to her while she's on her deathbed, praying she can still hear me. God, I don't feel good. If I could get my mind to come back inside my skull... but it's up there somewhere, watching us from the ceiling.

"Mrs. McLaughlin?" Nurse Anna pokes her head through the waiting room door. "Dr. Chen is ready for you now."

The woman Mommy was talking to looks at all three of us as we get up from our chairs. "Good luck," the woman says. Her words are right, but the way she's looking at us is dead wrong. Like we're heading in for a sentencing or a beheading.

Nurse Anna leads us through the short hallway to Dr. Chen's office and Anna gives my hand a squeeze. I love her. I love most of the nurses we've met over the last two and a half years. I want to tell her all the words that are jumbled up inside, but it's impossible to talk in a hallway on the way to an office, where Mommy is going to get important news and when you are half inside yourself and half outside yourself. I touch my pocket again. The feather and the pills are safe.

Dr. Chen's office is small and empty and not at all friendly. There are diplomas hanging on the wall near her desk. The top one is crooked but it would be really rude to straighten it, so I try not to look at it. There are dozens of file cabinets holding hundreds and hundreds of lives. Each manila folder holds a whole story. Mommy's story sits on top of Dr. Chen's desk.

There are always only two seats, so Mommy and Daddy sit while I stand behind them. I feel like a giant and I never know what to do with my hands, so I stick them in my pocket and grab hold of the feather.

"Mrs. McLaughlin," Dr. Chen says. "I know this is hard, so I'll avoid small talk and just get right to your scan results."

I hold the feather and touch my pills and wonder how my world will change, depending on what comes out of Dr. Chen's mouth. I close my eyes and wait.

♂OSS

I have a spritz in my hair for extra fruity shine. I'm wearing my really good jeans, the dark skinny ones, which are distressed at one knee. My makeup is fresh and classic, with a perfect cat-eye that took me twenty minutes of doing and redoing with my face pressed so close to the mirror that I was basically making out with it.

What I don't have is Malik's camera.

I forgot to even ask him to look for it after being with him on Monday. I can't stop thinking about our time together. It was a different plane. Maybe not so different from whatever the hell it is that Grandma's staring at all the time. It was a look at Beyond.

Malik promised he's going to bring the camera to me on his break from Sebastian's. Leo's going to give him a ride. All I have to do is get through until then. No problem. Armor-up, shield raised, no matter what Mr. Foster does to me, he won't be able to break through.

I'm not scared.

My whole life has prepared me for this. And maybe — *maybe* — Mom would be proud of me if she knew what I was about to do. I walk faster and faster toward Foster's classroom. *You'll never be the same,* Chloe had said to me, but that seems a small price to pay for justice.

I pull out my phone and text Malik.

You still coming to Raine with that camera? Need to put phone away for tutoring.

I know he won't answer. Not when he's on shift.

I'm close enough now that I see Foster leaning over his desk, grading papers. No book tie today.

"Hi," I say. I peek my head into the door.

"There you are! I was wondering."

I walk over to his desk. He'd pulled another chair up close to him. I throw the SAT book down in front of us. I move the chair even closer to him and then sit.

"So… just… you and me," I say.

"Better that way."

What does that mean? I could interpret it in seven hundred different ways.

My plan. My plan. Can I still stick to this when I don't have the camera yet? Aren't I now in the same position as everyone else at school? My word against his. A seventeen-year-old girl versus a white male English teacher with a Master's degree. Who are we kidding here? What did I actually think was going to happen?

Where's Malik? Where the *hell* is Malik? I check my phone again. No answer.

"Hey, hey! Remember what I said about —"

"Oh, yeah. I forgot."

Okay. Deep breath. Camera or no camera, Malik or no Malik.

"So," I say again. "Just us."

ⓑRYNN

Sebastian's Restaurant is painted in different shades of grey paint. The wall my parents and I sit near is a much darker shade than all the others. It reminds me a little of the mural at Raine High, like there's a storm rolling in. There's a pile of empty chairs stacked up against the wall. Joss's brother, Leo, pops in and out of the kitchen. I don't know if he knows who I am or not, which is super awkward, so I keep my head down and avoid eye contact.

It's only two o'clock in the afternoon, but Mommy and Daddy are drinking. Mommy says it's okay because there's orange juice mixed in with their champagne, so it's a drink that's meant for breakfast or lunchtime. I make my eyes give them this giant question mark as they clink glasses.

"Such a moral authority all the time," Daddy laughs at me. "Lighten up, Brynnie Brynn."

He's right. I should be celebrating. I raise my mug of hot chocolate along with their champagne glasses.

"To a clean scan," Mommy says.

We click our drinks together. My hot chocolate sloshes a little over the top and I take a big slurp to empty it a little.

"We need to thank God. It's not enough to just ask Him for things. We need to thank Him, too." Mommy turns to me. "Do you feel any better now? Do you think we were right in thinking this is what those panic attacks were about?"

No.

I don't feel better at all. It's so disappointing.

"So, back to school on Monday!" Daddy jumps right over Mommy's question. He tries to sound all casual, like he could just sneak it in there, as our server puts down plates of pancakes and omelets and a little dish filled with packets of butter and grape jelly. My parents are big fans of breakfast at all times of day. Lunch, dinner. Doesn't matter. Can't go wrong with pancakes and eggs.

"Anything else you need?" the server asks.

I sneak my eyes up at him and get a look at his name tag. *Malik*. Wow. *This* is Joss's boyfriend? He's cuter than I imagined. He's built like an athlete, but his face is soft and kind. I don't know if I should say anything or not about how I know Joss. Being this awkward is so much work that it's actually exhausting.

"Another round of mimosas?"

"Sure. We're celebrating," Daddy says.

"Clean mammogram."

"Mommy!"

"*Oh!*" Malik says. "Oh. My girlfriend mentioned… that her friend's mom… was going to be in Warden this afternoon." He turns to me. "Do you—um? Do you, by any chance, go to Raine High?"

"Do you know each other?" Daddy asks.

"Not really," Malik says and looks at Mommy. "Sorry. Um. Hey. Congratulations on the good news and everything. Mimosas on the house, okay?"

He backs away from the table, sort of shyly. Maybe he's just as uncomfortable as me.

"How do you know him?" Daddy asks.

"Joss's boyfriend."

"Jocelyn has a boyfriend? Does Charley have a boyfriend?"

"Charley doesn't—like she's not into that, I guess."

"Are you? Into it?"

I'm so tired. I don't want to laugh with them about having or not having a boyfriend.

Malik comes back with the drinks and puts them down on the table.

"Everything come out okay?"

"Hey," Daddy says, "So Brynn mentioned you know Jocelyn. That you and Jocelyn are going together."

"Going together?" Malik looks like he wants to crawl under the table.

"Daddy, no one like... says that."

"I'm sorry she couldn't join us for lunch," Mommy says. "That would have been fun. To have Charley and Jocelyn and Malik here to celebrate —"

"Oh, well, Joss's got English tutoring after school today. So, she couldn't have —" Malik starts to say.

"Tutoring?" I sit up really fast. My elbow slams against the bottom of the table.

"SAT. She wants to get her verbal and writing scores... I mean, I don't think she needs it. I'm bringing her a camera on break so she can record the sessions."

"A real camera? Like... from the 90s?" Daddy looks thrilled suddenly.

"Uh... no. Well. Not the *90s*. But still, it's very old."

"Mr. Foster hates cell phones," I whisper.

"Yeah! That's what she — hey. Are you okay?"

"She's panicking." Mommy jumps out of her seat and comes around to my chair. "Don't panic. Baby girl, panicking won't — and you didn't bring your pills, did you?"

I can't talk. I touch my coat pocket.

"Uh. What should we —? Should I call an ambulance?" I hear Malik ask.

"No, no," Daddy says. "This is par for the course."

"It is?"

"Though we had hoped that after today…"

They talk over my head, and that just makes it worse.

"What's going on?" Mommy asks me.

"Don't ask her that right now. Distraction is best for panic attacks. Brynn, can you find all the things in this room that are green? Let's count the green things."

I hear them, but I don't hear them. I see them, but I don't see them. Joss is in trouble. He'll do it to her, too. The hands will sneak down, down. Her waist. Her zipper. Her thigh. I see flesh. Fingers. Sweat. Fluorescent classroom lights.

"Air," I said. "I need —"

"Let's go outside," Mommy says. She pulls me up to standing.

I shake her off.

"By myself. Please," I say.

"You can't be by yourself right now! You're not thinking clearly."

"Just for a minute."

Daddy nods his head at Mommy. Let her, he says with his eyes. I leap up, turn around, and burst out the door. It rings when I push through it. An angel getting its wings. Isn't that what they say?

The sky is bright. The wind is angry. The air is cold.

I dig my hand into my pocket, grab the pill bottle, and dart away from the window to where Mommy and Daddy can't see me.

I could make it all go away. Not permanently. Not forever. Just a break. Just enough pills to wash these images away so that I sleep so deeply that I won't dream of witches or pink skin. Just enough pills to make the hands and the lights go away.

I open the bottle. I know I have only seconds before my parents come out to find me and drag me back inside to sing *Row, Row, Your Boat* or count colors or some other game for kindergarteners. *Dr. E.* Mommy had said. *Dr. E.* like I couldn't pronounce his real name. But I'm not a baby. Not anymore.

I pour a handful of pills into my hand.

The bells ring just as I pop the pills into my mouth.

"Whoa, whoa!" Malik rushes toward me. "What did you just take? What are you doing?" He sees the bottle in my hand and his eyes get bigger. "Spit those out right now."

I shake my head at him.

"Right *now,* and I'll take you with me. Me and Leo, we'll take you to school and you can be away from your parents for a little. That's what you want, right?"

Yes. That's all I need. A rest. A moment. If I can't get a full rewind, I at least deserve a pause button.

I spit the pills onto the ground. They sit there, dissolving on the pavement like wet chalk.

"Just a break," I whisper.

"Come on," Malik says.

The bell rings again, and Leo runs out. He's not wearing a coat. "Yo, we have like twenty-minutes before Caleb loses it that he's alone on shift. Let's go."

I walk with them and climb into Leo's car. Leo doesn't even ask why I'm getting in with them. Is this what normal people do? Just go along with things? Malik gives me the front seat. Leo flips the ignition on and pulls out from the curb. He barely watches where we're going.

I pull out my phone and text Mommy.

Going with Malik to bring Joss the camera.

Text bubbles pop up. She's typing furiously, but I don't want to know. I stick the phone back in my pocket before I can read her response. I stare out the window in silence. The wind bends the telephone wires and sends a rush of leaves tumbling through the parking lot.

"Hey, are you okay?" Malik asks.

Leo keeps one hand on the wheel and the other on the heat, turning the dial all the way up to blasting.

This is dangerous, I think. I'm not allowed to be in Leo's car.

"Better?" Leo asks me. "Warmer?"

Leo doesn't slow down when we get to a yellow light. I grip the door handle. But you know what? Is this any more dangerous than school? Is this any scarier than just living life every day, one second rolling on into the next? Kind teachers can be bad.

Strange college boys in wild cars can be good. You never know. You can never tell.

"My fault," I whisper.

"What's your fault? What are you talking about?" Malik asks from the backseat.

For the first time in my life, I'm too numb to cry. I watch the leaves tumble and crash into tires and cement. I think of Mommy, back at Sebastian's. She'll explode through the door and hurry toward the street, looking for Leo's car, looking for me, worrying about me. Alive, healthy, and whole, she'll take the sidewalk at a run. I love her so much; my heart might explode.

Mommy's safe, but Joss is in trouble. This is the universe balancing itself out. This is God's punishment. The hands and hands and hands. My silence. Joss taking it on herself to make things right. Joss paying for my inability to speak up. Mr. Foster, hurting her right now, as we fly through the streets.

"Faster, Leo," I say.

He revs the motor. Peels around a corner.

"What's your fault?" Malik asks again.

All of it; all of it, I think. Every last thing.

Joss

"Just us," Mr. Foster repeats. He flips the SAT book open to the back. "The most important part of doing well on the verbal section is your vocabulary. How's your vocab?"

I've lost all my vocab.

"Uh—it's—I don't know. It's fine."

"Since I don't know your work at all, why don't we start with a diagnostic test? There's a bunch of them in the back."

"Timed? I could time it on my phone!"

Nice, Joss. Not obvious at all.

"Or… I can time it. The very old-fashioned way. With my watch."

"Oh, oh. Okay."

"Go ahead."

"Start?"

"Yes, Jocelyn, go ahead and start."

I look down at the book. And just my luck, instead of the quicker vocab questions, it's this giant reading passage. I can barely make any sense of it at all. I just see these jumbled up words that are definitely supposed to mean something, but I'm so nervous, I can't get the words to form into sentences. I take a few deep breaths. Never mind. I'll skip to the questions. I go to number one.

Which choice best represents the main idea of the passage?

God. I have no idea. Literally, no idea.

I tap the end of my pencil against the book.

"Jocelyn," Mr. Foster says. "Are you feeling nervous?"

He puts his arm around my shoulders.

There it is. Right here. Right now. His arm is around my shoulders.

I'm so stupid. I'm the stupidest person who ever walked across the face of the earth. Why would I do this to myself? Who did I think I was? Some kind of hero, some kind of warrior? No. I'm Joss. Plain Joss. And I'm scared. And I can't breathe. And I want Grandma. I want Papa Bear. I want Mom or Leo or Malik. Anyone.

"Please, don't be nervous. I'm here to help you."

He rubs my arm. Up and down. Up and down. Up and down. Every hair on my body stands straight up. Like Brynn's cat. Like Willow.

"I feel—a little —sick," I say, when the classroom door bursts open.

Brynn.

I want to yell out her name but can't get myself to say anything. I can't say anything at all.

ᛒRYNN

"Oh no," Mr. Foster says to Joss. "You're not feeling well, huh?" His hands are around her shoulders.

Don't touch her, I scream, but only silently. *Don't you dare touch my friend.*

I hold on to the doorframe. Malik and Leo push in front of me and walk right into the classroom. Malik holds the camera in one hand.

I stay exactly where I am. I can't move.

"Hey!" Mr. Foster looks up. "Leonardo, your sister is —"

"Something's weird here," Malik says, sort of under his breath but loud enough that I hear him.

And okay, I'm a little in love with Malik for saying that out loud. I don't want him to be my boyfriend because I wouldn't do that to Joss. But it's like—how I used to want to mush into Charley all the time? It's the same feeling.

"Are you a student here?" Mr. Foster asks Malik. "You look very familiar."

"I was. I'm in college now."

"I'll take her to the nurse," Mr. Foster says.

"*We'll* take her to the nurse," Malik blurts out. He gestures at Leo and me.

"Oh, Brynn," Mr. Foster says. "Hello! I didn't see you there. How are you feeling? We've missed you in class. Mom doing okay?"

I can't think.

"Are *you* okay?" Mr. Foster asks me.

I see stars.

"Brynn?"

They're bright and shiny and filled with both terror and hope. *Twinkle twinkle* I sing in my mind, like Daddy would want me to do. My phone buzzes in my pocket. I'm sure it's Mommy or Daddy texting me again. My worlds are knocking in to each other like bumper cars.

"Something weird is going on here," Malik says again. He walks over to Joss and takes her hand. He pulls her up and guides Joss toward the door.

"Jocelyn, are you feeling better?" Mr. Foster calls after her.

She doesn't answer.

"Brynn, did you come to give me your essay?"

I don't answer.

Leo follows Malik and Joss toward the door. Then he puts his hand on my arm and guides me out of the room. Like Leo's my brother too. Like he's my friend.

Malik and Leo lead me and Joss away from the classroom, through the hall, beyond the bulletin board that advertises our winter concert. We go out the back door, outside to the fields, cut across the blue track, and go to the top of the bleachers. There's not a soul out here except for us. It's Friday. And it's freezing.

"What's going on?" Malik asks. "Start talking."

"Charley," I get myself to say.

The wind is crazy. I pull my ponytail out and try to smooth my hair back again. My white streak dips into my eyes. I grab it all and stick it into a bun.

"Librarian girl?" Leo asks.

"Get Charley," Joss agrees. "We need her now." Her voice is shaky and her face has no color, but her words are clear. "It's enough already."

And that's true. That's exactly right. Enough's enough.

CHARLEY

On Friday afternoon, I walk steadily through residential Raine and cross Main Street as quickly as I can, because I don't want to run into Ava coming into or out of the store. Though I don't have a plan, I'm filled with purpose, gravitating toward the pond like I'm pulled there by a long rope. The pond needs me or I need it. The rest will follow.

I pass the pizza restaurant where I had dinner with my parents the other night and A Scoop in Time, the ice cream place where the Ravens used to hang out after our pond picnics, back when there were five of us instead of one. Khadija's inside now. She hangs over the counter, talking to Julian, who works there after school. I try to pass the giant windows just as fast as I'd passed Jabberwocky, a dark shadow moving across the walk, a blur, but I'm not fast enough this time.

Khadija and Julian run out of the store. Call my name. I don't turn around.

"Hey, witch," Julian says. "Don't ignore us!"

"Charley," Khadija yells out. She says my actual name, which catches me off guard. I stop. "Charley, Emma is really sick. A fever, super sudden, out of nowhere. Like a lot of people have gotten sick who were in the hall with you yesterday. And we need to know what you did."

I laugh.

I didn't do anything to them. I'd raised my arms up into the air and let them draw their own conclusions.

"It's not funny, Charley!"

"Be careful," I say to her.

"Is that a threat?"

I shrug.

"I used to think you were a nice girl," Khadija says while Julian stands in front of her like a guard, like some kind of hero.

"So that's why you put feathers in my sandwich?"

"Get away from here," Julian says. "No one wants you here."

"No kidding."

I turn around and keep walking. Fast, fast, fast, a streak, a flash, until I'm around the corner, until I cross a final street, and pop out at a dead end block with a gravel path that will lead me through a small section of trees and then down to the pond.

There are snack wrappers and broken glass all over the path. A pile of beer cans cluster at the bottom of a tree. Some stupid kids must have found our spot. Ruined it. I hurry through the small grove and finally get to the edge of the pond. There's a strange, single yellow rain boot abandoned at the edge of the water.

I stare at that boot. I stare at it and I stare at it and suddenly I'm crouched on the ground, holding my stomach, not crying, more like howling, this sadness that lives in my stomach, an ancient sadness, pouring out, uncontainable, and I think about Julian's arms wrapped around Khadija like that, so safe, so warm, and how here I am, just me, no ducks, no bees, just the still water, nearly frozen.

I used to think you were a nice girl, Khadija had said.

I used to think so, too.

I yell out. And then I yell out again. It doesn't feel like my voice. It's a sound that's lived longer than me; a sadness older than time.

A bird screeches from a nearby tree.

I catch my breath.

Hello, I say. *Oh, hello.*

The raven screeches again; a greeting, a welcome. It's close, just above my head. Maybe it's back from the dead, or maybe it's brand new to this life. *Nevermore,* I think. *Nevermore.*

The poem about the raven makes me think of Dad. Dad who gave me books and poetry. Dad who showed me the path that dead black bird took: up, up, toward the moon.

I stand up, straighten up, crush a discarded cigarette with the sole of my boot.

The wind waltzes through the branches and whips my hair. I open my arms up wide to let the wind get inside my open coat. I let the chill get down to my bones.

My phone rings from inside of my pocket.

The sound is electronic and shrill, and it sucks me back into this life.

"Hello?" I say, as I shake my head. "Hello?"

There's static. The Raven screams from its tree. I cover one ear with my palm and adjust my feet, which have gone numb from standing in the dirt.

"Hello?" I say again.

"Charley," a voice says. "Your friends need you."

"Friends?"

"Please come to your school."

The wind won't let up. It lashes at my coat.

"Charley, are you listening to me?"

"Who is this?"

"Malik Jones."

"What's the matter?"

"I have to go."

"Wait —"

"Just come."

"Please—stay on the phone with me?"

But he's already gone and I'm alone again.

I turn from the pond and run back through the trees, toward where the people are. Toward the warmth of them and away from the cold. The raven laughs at me. It tries to call me back.

·   ·   ·

I know what I look like. Crazed, a wanderer, a witch, appearing on the bleachers like a spirit summoned by a woman with a crystal ball. One minute at the pond, the next, here, by the fields, *poof, abracadabra.* I know how my hair looks. Windblown, a twig stuck in it, dressed head to toe in black.

"Thanks for coming," Malik says. "I'm Malik. I—called you."

"I know who you are."

"Did you do something to my sister?" Leo asks me. "Did you make her go in there for some reason?"

"Calm down," Malik says to him.

"Go in there? Go in where?" I pause for a second. Stand straight up. "What did you do to him?"

"Please don't talk to Joss like that," Malik says to me. "She didn't do *anything.*"

"They're right. I did nothing," Joss says. "I'm a total failure."

"Seriously. What's going on? Were you really doing SAT tutoring?" Leo asks his sister.

"Your plan failed because of me," I say to Joss. "Banishing spell. I did it to protect you."

"You did it to protect *him.*"

"Both of you."

"Your spell isn't why these guys came when they did."

"Of course it is."

"You're so stupid."

"So, you really are a witch?" Leo says to me and then looks at Joss. "What are you doing hanging out with her, Jocelyn? I *told* you that you were going to get sucked into her cult. Come on. Get in the car. Brynn too."

"There are a lot of things about your sister that you don't know, huh?" I say.

"Stop it, Charley," Joss says.

"It's okay," Malik says. "Whatever Charley has to say. It's okay."

"Joss's an empath," I blurt out. "She's a Raven."

"*You're* a witch?" Leo says to Joss.

"No! I mean. I don't know. I just- all I know is, I thought I could stop Mr. Foster. I thought I could do it by myself, without you guys. Without Mei or Chloe. But then I couldn't. I got scared. Just like a little kid. A pathetic little baby."

I think about that for a second. Joss—scared. That doesn't make sense. It's not something I can imagine, even with all the hundreds of books I've read about characters changing, growing, becoming more or different from who they were on page one.

"You were scared?"

"Yes, Charley. I was terrified."

"Of what?"

"You know of what. You *know*. Don't you?"

I take a deep breath.

"Did he… did he try?" I ask. "To hurt you?"

Joss looks at me for a long time. They all do, like they're trying to see right through me.

"He was going to, Charley. He was about to."

"Are you sure?"

"I'm sure."

I go crashing down to the bleachers. The boys stare at me. Joss grabs my hand. "I'm really, really, sorry," Joss says to me.

"You're not the one who has anything to be sorry about."

"I feel awful for you. Even with my… you know. My shield. It's easy to see how much this… we all — we all care about you!"

"I'm as bad as he is."

"Never."

"So, this really is the end, then."

"It's — it's more like the beginning, right?" Joss asks.

She's right, I'm sure, though the beginning of *what* is something that's hard to let myself understand right now. For now, for a few seconds more, I hug my knees and close my eyes against the wind and the voices that circle. *Beware, Charley, careful, Charley.* And when I open them again, and see Brynn and Joss and Malik and Leo, all still standing beside me, I know that it's time, finally, to listen.

฿RYNN

Charley sinks down, so she's sitting on the bleacher. Joss grabs her hand. They talk about ends and beginnings and Charley shuts her eyes up tight. And I want to be with them, at this place of new beginnings they're talking about, but I'm stuck back there, back a few beats now, classic Brynn, a little slower to catch on, but still...

"I just — I don't understand. You wanted him to hurt you?" I say to Joss. I'm shaking. My arms right down to my legs.

"Nothing happened, Brynn," Charley's voice drifts from her seat, her eyes open again. Classic Charley. The first one to take care of me when anyone can see that she's the one who needs to be taken care of right now. "Joss's okay. See?"

"I'm not fine," Joss says. "You're not fine. Brynn is definitely not fine. None of us are fine!"

My phone vibrates again. Mommy. I touch my pocket where the pills were before Malik took them.

Mommy's texts make me remember everything that happened this morning.

"My mom's still cancer-free," I suddenly whisper. "The mammogram was good. So I had to be punished somehow else instead. For doing witchcraft."

"Punished?" Malik asks.

"She means Mr. Foster," Joss says.

"Wait. Did he hurt *you*?" Malik asks me. "What's going on?"

I don't say anything. I don't say anything. I don't say anything. But somehow, Malik knows anyway.

"I'm so, so sorry," he says.

And it's the first time. It's the first time at all that anyone has said something like that to me.

"But that isn't your fault," Malik continues. "Do you hear me? It's not your fault."

I take his words in. I hold them close to me like small flowers bursting out of concrete. The feeling is warm and good and—big. It surrounds me. A warmth. A glimpse of Beyond.

Joss opens her mouth to say something but then shuts it again. She looks at Malik and gives him some kind of signal with her eyes.

"Let's let them talk," Malik says to Leo.

The guys get up and head down the bleachers. They hit the track and keep going, jogging toward Leo's car. "We'll wait for you!" Leo calls back to us. And that's really nice, too. To be waited for.

In another minute, they're gone, and it's just the three of us, the way it used to be.

"Malik's right. It wasn't Brynn's fault," Joss says. "It was all of us. It was The Ravens."

For a second, my breath catches in my lungs and I feel the panic take hold. But no. My phone still vibrates in my pocket. Mommy is checking in on me from the restaurant again. Mommy, whose cancer has *not* come back. Malik and Leo are in the car. Charley and Joss, my best friends, are right here. They're right *here*.

"No." I stand up. "I think...maybe... it was none of us. It was him. It was Foster." I turn to Charley. "Your dad."

My friends are good people who only want to do what's right. They only wanted to do something big and beautiful to help the world. And I realize. I suddenly understand. *Click*, a light switch thrown on. I'm a good person too. Everything I ever learned in Catholic school about an angry God was wrong. Everything I read a few nights ago about God punishing me was wrong. I feel it. A hand not pointing from above, but a finger guiding me. Helping me. Telling me: If this isn't my friends' fault, then it can't possibly be my fault either.

"This is the year we rise," I whisper.

"How?" Joss asks. "How, how, how, how, *how*?"

I don't answer. I take their hands and look at them for a minute. Joss looks pale and sick. Charley is clenched up and wild looking, all in black, with that stick still stuck in her hair. But even still. They are beautiful and they're strong. And they're mine.

I feel snapped to attention. The panic is — not gone, exactly. How could it be? But it's buried. It's shoved away somewhere.

"We're going to speak up," I say. "We're going to turn him in."

"Brynn. Brynn, I'm so scared," Charley says.

"I'm scared, too."

We don't take out our feathers. We don't have any crystals. But it doesn't matter. Maybe it's never mattered. There's no actual plan, and no words left to say, so I just sit there and hold on to their hands for dear life. We stay like that for a long time. Our tiny circle of friends.

ℐOSS

After our afternoon out on the bleachers, Leo's not talking to me. And I mean, it's—whatever. I don't care. It's not like we have these deep chats all the time, and I miss his philosophical outlook on life or anything.

He says nothing. Nothing, nothing, nothing. Just sits on the couch across from Grandma in her armchair. He's waiting for Mom to come so they can go off on some adventure together. Leo and Grandma both stare out the window. The TV is on. I don't remember who turned it on or when, but I have a feeling it's been on for like three days, the entire weekend, with no one bothering to click the button on the remote. The sound is company, I guess, now that Leo isn't.

"You've gotta talk to me. You're driving me crazy."

Nothing.

"So *what* if I didn't tell you about the Ravens stuff? Like I'm so sure you tell me everything about your life all the time."

Silence.

"Do you want to know why I wanted Malik's camera?"

Maybe if I don't shut up, same as the TV, Leo will eventually tune in and come back to me.

"You know when we study bad stuff in history class? I always think, *oh my god why didn't anyone do anything*? And so, I tried to do something, but it was a really, really stupid thing. And I sort of knew that. That it was dumb."

Nothing.

"Do you think staying quiet about it made me as bad as Charley? Mei and Chloe said that it was just as terrible as Charley. Is that why you're not talking to me? Does this make me as bad as Mr. Foster, even? Am I a bad person?"

Silence.

"Leo —" I choke out, but there's no way to end that sentence. It's bottomless.

I cry. I cry and I cry and I cry and it's the first time in years. I'm like those cowards at school who don't know how to be brave, be strong, stand up straight, or have their *warrior modes activated*.

And it's right now, because, of course, it is, because I have all the luck in the world, that the front door opens and Mom pushes her way into the living room.

God, I can't believe it. I haven't cried like this in years. And now here I am being a total baby, just like I was when I was a little kid. She won't understand that I'm different now. A fighter. A warrior. But none of that seems to matter because I can't get myself together. I can't stop crying.

"Oh, sweetheart," she says.

Sweetheart. A baby word, but still.

She comes over to me. Sits right down next to me on the damn floor.

"Ignore me. Ignore me. Just — go with Leo. It's all good."

"Did your brother say something to you? Or is something going on with your friends? What's —"

"I'm sorry. I'm so sorry that I'm —"

"What on earth do you have to be sorry for? There's *nothing* to be sorry for."

"I'm being such a baby. Just. Go. With him. Do whatever you were going to do. He's not talking to me anyway, so he's really bad company." I point to my brother. My brother who doesn't care about school while I'm going to be an engineer someday. It's not fair. It's not just. "And I mean, whatever. You always choose him. And I know it's because I used to cry too much and I wasn't strong like you guys were. But I am now. I know you don't believe me when I look like this, but I swear I'm different now. I know how to not feel anything. Like turn it all off."

"Please never turn it off. I didn't know. I had no idea, even, that you—I was trying to protect you. That's all. I thought I was protecting you from things that seemed to hurt you so much."

"Mom?"

She puts her hand on my back.

It's good to be independent. It's good to be strong. It's good to be fast. To race on to the next big thing. But I'm also so scared. And that's the real live truth.

"Jossie." A voice. Not Mom's. Not Leo's.

Grandma sits straight up in her chair.

I see infinity, but backwards. I see a flash of her giant suitcase in our living room and the way our kitchen smelled sweet when the oven was hot and the dough was rising.

"Grandma?" I wipe my eyes, get up, and kneel at her feet. I take her hands in mine. "Grandma, can you hear me?"

"Jossie," she says again and moves her hand to my face.

As long as that suitcase was in the living room, I knew I could get up early and run to her room and that she would braid and rebraid my hair while we watched the news. *You can tell me anything, Jossie,* she had said. *Anything, anything.*

"I've missed you," I say to her now. "I've missed you so much."

I see the water against the sand on the shore. The indentation of seashells after Leo and I plopped them into our bucket. The dolphins, further out, beyond the waves. The spoon and the sauce and the meatballs on the baking sheet.

"You look so beautiful. My beautiful granddaughter."

"My beautiful grandmother."

She smiles. Her eyes are bright. I see years in them.

"I love you," I say. "We all —"

"Oh," she says. "Oh, yes?"

"Yes," I repeat. "Yes, definitely!"

"I'm so proud of you," she says.

"You are?"

She doesn't answer.

"Grandma? Do you really mean that? Grandma? Hey, Grandma?"

But she's staring at whatever it is she sees when she's not with us.

I turn away from Grandma and see that Mom and my brother are looking at me. Mom's got tears in her eyes. Look at that. Mom crying.

"That was —" I say, but then stop. "Where do you think she goes?"

As I look at her, I suddenly think of physics class. And how energy is neither created nor destroyed. "She's got like this whole other life inside of her. I know it. She knows things we'll never be able to — but — did you see that, Leo? Did you see it?" I ask.

It was a second — just one second — but I felt the energy of the universe shifting and unfolding all around us.

"I saw it," he says quietly.

It's the first time he's spoken to me since he found out about The Ravens. His whisper is the size of a mountain.

I get up and click off the TV and then settle back onto the floor with Mom.

"I need to tell you something," I say. "I need to tell you… a lot of things. It's a long story."

"We have time."

And that's true. There's no need to rush. There's no need to run, to fly, to be carried off on an impossible quest with my red sneakers blazing.

I take a deep breath.

"There's a teacher at school," I begin. "This is… difficult to say."

"But you're brave."

And I am. I. Am. So. Brave.

"He's a terrible man."

"Oh, sweetheart."

Sweetheart, she'd said.

She takes my hand. I let the tears come.

BRYNN

Monday. English class.

Mr. Foster has the screen pulled down and the lights off. A giant bag of popcorn sits on his desk next to a stack of paper bowls. Khadija goes up there and starts pouring the popcorn out. She makes neat rows of snacks across Mr. Foster's desk.

"Thanks for the popcorn, Mr. F.," Mason calls from the back. "You're our new favorite teacher."

A couple of my classmates agree with him and add their thanks for the popcorn and the movie. Mei and Chloe, who sit to my left, don't say anything, but I catch them giving each other a look.

"Ian McKellen is an iconic Macbeth," Mr. Foster says. "This is the best version out there, in my opinion."

"Probably the oldest version, too," Khadija says from up front.

"Old doesn't mean without value. Does it?"

"You keep telling yourself that, Mr. F."

It's a lonely feeling when my classmates talk and joke with Mr. Foster like he's a good man. A favorite teacher. It's even more awful when the other two girls who could expose him for what he is don't know to include me in their secret looks.

I don't know if my stomach is upset because of what Mr. Foster did to me, or if I'm sick because I haven't *told* anyone about what he did to me. All of those words piled up and up inside, bursting. Ready.

I stand.

"You okay, Brynn?" Mr. Foster asks. "Not going to faint on us, are you?"

His eyes are kind. Disgusting. That's probably the most disgusting part.

The words are almost here. I feel them behind my closed lips, but my stomach lurches and I run down the aisle toward the door. All twenty-four sets of eyes watch.

"So, does this mean I can have her popcorn?" Mason asks.

I whip around to face him. Asshole.

"Where are you going?" Mr. Foster asks.

I say nothing, but my eyes are daggers. They're *daggers*.

"She's sick," Mei suddenly says. "She feels sick."

"I'm very sorry to hear that. Can you please hand me your revised essay before you go to the office?"

"No," I say.

"What?"

"She said no." Mei stands and joins me at the front of the room. She waves for Chloe to follow. Chloe looks terrified. Her face is ghost white. But Mei motions to her again and this time Chloe gets up and joins us at the front of the room.

"Are you... are both of you taking Brynn to the office?"

There's a flash of fear in Mr. Foster's eyes. It's gone in a matter of seconds, but it was there and that's something. It's something big.

"Ladies?"

"Yes, Mr. Foster, we're both taking her," Mei says. "Is that a problem?"

"I just don't think all three of you need to —"

"Well, maybe you should have thought of that earlier," Mei says. "If you're so worried about us going to the *office*."

"Girls?"

His eyes are in a full-on panic, like a little kid instead of a teacher. Good. We're in charge now.

We leave the room in silence. The revolution's begun.

•   •   •

We can hear the movie play from the hall.

"Come away from there." Mei gestures toward the end of the hall and Chloe and I follow her. We walk down the corridor until we get around the bend and out of sight of Mr. Foster's door. Once we're safely around the corner, I put my backpack on the ground and lean against a bulletin board advertising our winter concert. We stare at the ground for a minute. I didn't know revolutions could be so uncomfortable.

"Think Khadija's gonna get the solo again?" Chloe asks. She traces her finger over a cutout of a snowflake. The bulletin board looks like an elementary school teacher designed it instead of a high school teacher. That kind of thing embarrasses me. It reminds me of the Urgent Care doctor treating me like a little kid.

"What a stupid bulletin board." I point to a picture of a smiling snowman. "We're not first-graders."

"I know, right?" Chloe giggles. I've missed her. She's a little awkward, like me. "May as well have stuck a picture of the Ice Queen up there. My three-year-old cousin is beyond obsessed."

"The movie's kind of good, though," I say.

"Oh, my God. Thank you for saying that. It's *so* good!" Chloe laughs. Yeah, she's definitely awkward.

Mei, on the other hand, is more serious. She stands in the middle of the hall with both arms crossed over her chest. She has a little tattoo on her wrist. I'd never noticed it before.

"Your parents let you get that?" I ask her, rubbing my wrist to show her I'm talking about her tattoo. "What is it?"

"It's a Japanese character. It means *strength*."

"My parents would never let me."

"Well, next year, when you turn eighteen, they can't decide stuff like that for you anymore."

"Actually, I'm pretty sure they'll still be making decisions for me when I'm like thirty-six with a husband and a kid."

"So," Chloe interrupts. "What are we doing?"

"Do you want to talk about it?" Mei asks. "Joss already told us. You know. About what happened."

"But you don't have to," Chloe says quickly. "Joss *shouldn't* have told us."

"And she shouldn't have cornered us like that either," Mei adds.

"I think she knows that now," I say. "Did you tell Principal Suarez? Charley thought that maybe when you left in the middle of chorus the other day, you —"

"Ms. Suarez told us we misread the situation," Chloe says. "She loves Mr. Foster."

"Everybody loves Mr. Foster," Mei adds. "That's how they get you. By being so nice."

"They?"

"It's everywhere. It's absolutely everywhere. And it has to end."

I want to trust them. I want to trust them so badly.

"How come you — why did you all make fun of us with those feathers?"

"We told Charley about her dad, and instead of helping us, she kicked us out of the group."

"I think *she* needs help. You know?"

"Our help?"

"Like we all—us girls. We need to stick together."

"Us skein girls?"

"No." It's obviously not normal—*so* not normal — for me to take charge of anything. But Joss and Charley already had a shot at this, so now, it might as well be me. Why not me? *Fake it till you make it*, Daddy always says, and now I think there might be something to that, because something really weird is happening to me.

Last Friday afternoon, when the three of us were outside on the bleachers, my anxiety had suddenly lifted a little and I could see really clearly, like I hadn't known I was half-blind until just that moment. I can see now that everything around us is spinning out of control. Nothing around us makes sense. But *we* make sense. The five of us. Me, Joss, Charley, Mei, and Chloe. We're the center of the vortex. We're the eye of the hurricane, like the break in gray paint on the mural in the gym.

"No, not skein girls. *Ravens*. The five of us, together. So we can take a stand. So we can say it out loud."

We're quiet for a few seconds. Chloe continues tracing the snowflakes with her index finger.

"You know something?" Mei says suddenly. "That white in your hair? It looks like fire."

A spark has been lit. That's true enough. Maybe it's been here all along. It's hard to know. But it kindles now, slow and soft, steady and bright.

"Joss told her mom this weekend. About everything that happened."

"She *did*?"

"And her mom wants to talk to Ms. Suarez, but —"

"Ms. Suarez won't believe her. That's why we need Charley! That's why we've always needed Charley."

"Then we'll get Charley," I say. "We'll tell our parents, we'll get Charley to back us up, and we'll take him down."

The bell rings.

"Okay?" I say, as the halls start to fill.

"Okay," Mei and Chloe say together.

Soon, there are dozens of students racing through the halls and opening and closing lockers. Their laughter is loud and light, soaring over our heads.

"Hey, you three, move. Wake up," a senior guy says, barreling into us with a hockey bag and giant backpack.

There's no way he could know this, of course, but I've never been more awake.

Joss

There's frost on the trees and a little ice that crunches beneath Malik's and my feet as we jog through the park. Our breaths are pieces of ripped up clouds.

"I. Am. So. Tired," I say. "Need a break."

Malik taps his phone to get a look at his running app. "We literally just started! We've done less than half a mile. Come on!"

He pulls my hand and I laugh. You can see my laugh hanging in the air like a fairy. We get onto the path and skid across a very thin layer of ice. We startle a squirrel so that it runs into a nearby tree.

"A bench!" I yell and come to a complete stop. "Hey, look! A bench. Look how beautiful it is. Just calling out or names to come and sit on it."

"Ugly bench," Malik says. "Ugliest bench I've ever seen."

"Beauty is in the eye of the beholder. Come on, pleaaase!" I plop myself down.

"What are you doing?" he calls out, then comes back to me and sits.

"You mad?"

"I can't get mad at you."

"Not even when I don't tell you I'm a witch for six whole months?"

"*Are* you a witch?"

"Don't know."

"Well, how about this, then? Truth or Dare?"

Using my own game against me, huh?

"Truth. It's always Truth. You know that."

"Okay. So… are you a witch? Honestly."

"I don't know."

"I don't see how you could not know."

"It's complicated."

"Try me."

I think for a few seconds.

"It depends on your definition of witch, I guess."

"Have you ever done a spell?"

"I mean, I've helped cast… I've done stuff with Charley. At the pond. Me and Brynn and Chloe and Mei had this like… group."

"A coven?"

"We never called it that. We just called it —"

"The Ravens."

"Yeah. That."

"Okay," Malik says.

"But like, I never *wanted* to do any of that stuff. You know? I kept telling Charley that it was so stupid and that I didn't believe it. You can even ask her. She'll tell you. I hated it."

"Then why did you hang out with them?"

"See, this is the part I'm scared to tell you. I don't want you to think I'm crazy."

"I already think you're crazy."

"Oh, HA, HA, HA. You're hilarious."

"I'm not like…" He shifts around on the bench so that he faces me. "Listen to me, Jocelyn Esposito. I'm not going anywhere anytime soon. You can trust me."

"But… the mirror," I say really quickly. I hadn't known I was going to bring that up until the words just exploded right out of my mouth.

"Huh?"

"Last time we played Truth… I saw you in the mirror. Us. Together, in the future. But you didn't see me. You saw — like — you said you only saw darkness."

"That's what you've been worried about?"

"So worried!"

"But that's not about you. It's about me."

"Okay, that's the most classic cliché ever, and I'm actually really embarrassed for both of us that you just said that out loud."

"I'm being serious. The mirror was… Look. You didn't want me to think you're crazy. I don't want you to think I'm crazy, either."

"But I don't! I wouldn't! I just want to *know* you. Know more about you than that you're a great runner and that you hate calculus and that you look really… like… *really* good in glasses."

Malik kisses my forehead, and we can just stop this whole conversation. I don't even care. I just want him to kiss me like that again, even though I'm sweaty and gross.

But instead, he says, "I have bad days. Sometimes."

"We all have bad days."

"No. I mean that I have bad days the way that Brynn has bad days. Can't get out of bed bad days. Ever since my mom… died. I've felt this way. And then I just left my dad. When I should be there to keep him company."

"It's not your job to protect your dad."

Malik gives me this long look and I catch myself. I'm a hypocrite. Yeah, I get it.

"But anyway, those really terrible days? That's why I could talk to Brynn on Friday. I get it. The guilt. I get where she's coming from."

There's something in his voice. So much sadness. Like a cave that goes on and on.

"I've always known that you're sad," I say. "That's not a surprise to me. And it definitely doesn't make me think you're crazy."

"It doesn't bother you? The depression?"

"No! I want to help you!"

"Just be with me, Joss. That's enough."

"That's all?"

"That's all. Now get up! We'll slow down, set a steady pace, but let's keep going. It's good for you."

Keep going, huh? Slow and steady, right? Up till now, that hasn't been my style.

"Okay, but like for how long?"

"Infinity!"

"Infinity?!"

He kisses my hand and then jogs again. Though his pace isn't fast, his legs are pretty long, and he's already way ahead of me. His feet pound into the path.

"Hey! Hey!" I yell. "Wait up!"

"Gotta catch me."

I start jogging again. A hot mess. I can't stop laughing.

"Hey Joss," Malik calls back to me. He's running backward now. Show-off.

"I'm going to murder you. When I catch you."

"It's *you*, you know!" he yells out.

"It's me *what?*"

"In the mirror. I see you."

The sun is bright and glinting against the cold ground. Like fire. Like we'd called it down just for us, just for me and Malik. I run faster. Push my jelly legs hard. He stops and waits for me and when I finally catch up, he gives me a sweaty kiss.

"Oh, look," I say, after Malik pulls away. "Another bench!"

"Amazing that it should just appear here like that. Out of thin air."

"I guess we shall have to sit on it. Every time we see a bench, we'll sit on it. Deal?"

"What a coincidence, that so many benches should keep popping up in the *park*."

"Not everything's a coincidence," I say.

"Well, luck then. It's your lucky day."

He pulls me toward the bench. The air is cold, but his hand is warm and the sun is bright. It's sort of funny, the way things can be cold and hot at the same time. The middle ground. The shades of gray Charley told me about.

My burning legs are really, really grateful to be sitting. I'm definitely not used to endurance running yet, but Malik will coach me.

"No," I say. "No. Not luck."

"Well, what is it then?"

"I'll never tell."

"So mysterious! Come on. Just tell me."

"My lips are sealed."

"I'll help you unseal them." He kisses me again. "Did that help?"

"Nope. Better try it again."

He does, and it's electric. Kinetics. Physics. "Now?"

"Still not going to say."

But it's magic, I think. It's magic.

ᛒRYNN

Some places that seemed really giant when I was a kid look small now. It's always a little sad to realize that some places are only big when you're small. But A Scoop in Time? It's still giant. It's exactly as I remember it, with freezers full of every ice cream flavor a person can dream up and rows of toppings with little purple spoons sticking out. There's every topping from the normal fresh fruit and crushed cookies to crazy things like crystalized ginger and edible lavender.

"Too many choices!" Joss says, as she leans over the freezer. "My head's going to explode."

"We all have to try a new flavor. That's the rule," I say.

Julian is behind the counter. He can't roll his eyes any higher without them twisting completely around and getting stuck somewhere inside his brain. A few months ago, that would have really bothered me, but now I don't care. Let him roll his eyes. What on earth does it matter?

"I just want Cookies and Cream," Charley says quietly.

"Nope, nope, nope."

"Look at you, making the rules!" Joss says to me. "I like that, Brynn." She turns to Julian, who's stopped rolling his eyes and started giving us death stares instead. "We'll try every flavor, please."

"You can't do that," Julian says.

"Says right there we can," Joss points to a sign behind his head. She says it half flirty and half mean. I think I'd like to learn how to do that.

"Says you can try *a* flavor before buying it."

"Every flavor!" Joss says. "Can't waste our money, now, can we, Julian?"

He gives a really dramatic sigh and starts sticking the purple spoons into the fat tubs of ice cream. He passes them over the counter to us and we try flavors at the beginning of the alphabet like Blueberry Basil and Bacon Brittle before moving on to Doughnut ice cream and Maple and finally Thai Tea and Toasted Almond.

"We'll take three vanillas," I say to Julian.

"Brynn!" Joss bursts out laughing.

Charley is quiet beside us. It's like the world has gotten all shaken up and turned upside down.

Julian looks at us as if he would use an unforgiveable Harry Potter curse.

"Hey, Voldemort," Joss says to him. "The vanillas, please."

"I was just *thinking* he looks like Voldemort!" I say to Joss. "I can't believe you just said that."

"And you think you don't have ESP like we do?"

My breath catches for a second as Julian hands over our plain dishes and we dig some money out. How did Joss know that?

We take our ice cream over to a window seat and settle into our chairs. The dessert is sweet and good and even in the dead of winter, I think of summer. I think of my cousins playing on the swing set in my yard during summer break and the way they'd tell me stories about their friends from school. I used to make up stories about my classmates, so I had something to say to them. *When Sophie and I went to the zoo*, I would say, or *when I went to Kaylee's house...*

But the lies had made me lonely. I had felt separate from my cousins. There was always something between us that made it impossible to connect.

"You guys?" I say, as I dip my spoon deep into the cup, "Joss is right. I—I'm not really an empath."

Charley and Joss look up from their dessert. They don't say anything for about a hundred years. They look at each other instead of me. My God, I wish they would say something.

"Okay," Joss finally says. "I mean, I already knew that, really."

"Okay?" I repeat. "Charley?" My first friend. Her hair is loose today and hangs in crazy waves around her face. Her freckles are a compass, same as always. They're a straight path that leads from her forehead to her chin. But something about her is different. Duller. "I still want to be a Raven," I say quickly. "It's—that's why I hadn't told you before."

"I'm so sorry," she says, and lowers her eyes. "I'm sorry I forced The Ravens on you."

"Oh my God, you definitely didn't force me to join The Ravens."

"You were worried your mom wouldn't like the rituals we were doing for her, and I didn't listen to you."

"It was my choice to do them. And it worked! But it was *you*. That's what I'm saying. You guys saved my mom. I don't—like—I've never believed it enough to be any good at it. Or I wasn't born the same way you and Joss were."

"There's no such thing as magic," Charley says. "It was all just in my head this whole time."

"Charley —" Joss starts to say.

"I'm sorry for the stupid rules." Charley interrupts Joss. "I'm sorry I said you couldn't—I tried to stop you from dating Malik. Just because I don't care about boys doesn't mean you shouldn't get to care about them either. It's obvious you should be with him. He's—like he's a really great person."

"*Of course,* there's magic," Joss says. "*Of course,* there is."

Charley looks at Joss for a long time. Looks up at her with these really sad eyes. Then the bells over the door jingle and Mei and Chloe walk in. I hadn't told Charley or Joss that I was going to invite them, because I knew they would both say no. But they have to be here. I see it. I see it maybe the way Charley used to see things, when she believed in magic.

"Hey, guys." I wave them over.

"What are they doing here?"

Mei and Chloe pull over some more chairs and sit down with us. Julian gives our table even more death stares when they sit without ordering anything.

"I don't see why he should care," I say, nodding toward Julian. "It's not like he makes a commission on ice cream sales."

"He's just a generally grumpy person," Chloe answers, instead of saying hi to everyone. "He should try getting up on the wrong side of the bed. The right side of the bed is obviously not working if this is his go to personality."

"'Chlo-losophy'," Mei says.

"It's going to be offered as a major at NYU next fall."

"Literally all she talks about is NYU."

"My dad went to —" Charley says, but then stops.

Joss suddenly acts like her ice cream is the most interesting thing she's ever seen. She leans down close and examines it.

"Hey," Charley says. "I didn't mean to just like-bring him up all casually like that. I'm still trying to get used to the—to the idea."

"So, you believe us now?" Mei asks.

"I'm really, really sorry about kicking you girls out. I—I know what I have to do, but..." "We're going to go to the police, Charley," Chloe says. "Instead of Ms. Suarez. Me, Mei, Joss, and Brynn. When Brynn tells her parents. Which she will. She *will*." She gives my hand a squeeze. "And we need you with us, Charley. We need all five of us together."

"I'm so scared," Charley says. And I think that this is the first time I've ever heard *Charley*. Just regular, stripped-down Charley. No feathers. No crystals. No salt. Her real voice is beautiful and sad.

"You think Harry Potter wasn't scared when he took down Voldemort?" Joss motions toward Julian, who is still giving us evil looks from across the store.

"While we're admitting things," I say, "I've never read the books. Only seen the movies."

"Whaaaaaat?" The light pops briefly back into Charley's eyes.

"Jabberwocky?" Chloe asks. She points across the street.

"I can't go in there. I quit my job the other day. Never even told you guys."

"Come on. Get up," Joss says and pulls Charley to her feet. "It's basically an emergency that we buy *Sorcerer's Stone* right now. A *book* emergency, Charley."

"Okay," she whispers.

It's decided. We push in our chairs and toss our napkins into the trash. Mei and Joss chat about engineering programs while Chloe fills Charley in on the village and NYU's giant library.

"Apparently," Chloe says, "They named their school mascot after their library's card catalogue and came up with the name bobcats. It's the nerdiest thing I've ever heard."

"Nerdy is perfect for me," Charley says.

We leave our empty dishes on the table and all of us: one, two, three, four, five girls — march out into the cold.

CHARLEY

Seeing Ava on the stage with the spider and pig puppet cracks my heart in half. We make eye contact and Ava smiles at me. It's a sad smile —Ava isn't capable of a big old grin —but it's not a mad one. I could float away on that smile. I've missed her so much. I've missed her *so* much. Like always, I'm overcome with the feeling that I want to hug her pain away. I want to swallow it all up for her and hold it in me, the same way I now hold Brynn and Mei and Chloe's shame as if it were my own.

But none of that is real, I remind myself. All of that is imagined. There's no such thing as empathy. There's no such thing as ravens appearing and disappearing into thin air. The moon has never talked to me. These were just things I'd invented so I wouldn't have to face the fact that my dad is a dangerous man. That without meaning to, I sided with him and that makes me bad too. There's no such thing as magic.

Ava keeps reading to the kids, and I show Brynn and the other girls where the Harry Potter books are.

"I'm so jealous," I say to Brynn, though my mind is really elsewhere. "I wish I could read them for the first time again."

"That's an oxymoron, isn't it? Though I'm never really sure what oxymoron means," Chloe says. "It sounds like it means dumb ox."

"NYU will also offer a minor in Chloe's word origins," Mei says.

"Chlo-rigins," Brynn says. "I'd totally take that class."

I never realized that Brynn is funny.

The girls keep talking about different made-up majors and then split up and wander around the teen section. A couple of the little kids' parents drift around, pulling books off of the shelves and consulting lists on their phones. The store will be busy from now until Christmas, which is an excellent thing. Ava once told me she makes half her profit for the entire year in December. I hope the store will stay afloat. I hope the big chains and online shopping won't wash it away because yes, of course, the prices are higher, but you don't get Ava in a chain bookstore. You don't get her wise Charlotte or her timid Wilbur anywhere else but here.

Ava puts down the book and puppets and the children scatter, running back to their parents or to the shelves of stuffed animals, which I know the kids are going to throw everywhere. I guess Ben's the one who has to put them back now. Who knew I'd ever miss cleaning up the store?

"It's so good to see you," Ava says and pulls me into a giant hug. Her braids brush against my cheek. "How are you?"

I pull back and pick up her pentacle between two fingers. The quartz is pretty and pale. I'm so sad. I'm just so, so incredibly sad. Not Ava's sadness. Not Brynn's or Joss's, but mine.

The other girls come close and stand awkwardly around us.

"And you must be Charley's friends," Ava says. "I've heard a lot about you."

"This is Joss," I say. "And — well, this is Brynn. And Mei and Chloe."

"Oh!" Ava says. "Hi, girls. Hi." And the way she says it? All of them realize Ava *knows* at the same time. "Finding everything you need?"

"She's never read Harry Potter." I point to Brynn. "It was 911."

"Well, that *is* urgent," Ava laughs.

"What's your favorite book?" Chloe asks. "I'm always asking for expert advice. The stuff we read at school is the worst."

"*To Kill a Mockingbird*'s 'the worst'? *Macbeth*'s 'the worst'?" I put my hand to my forehead like I'm about to faint.

"Charley and I are on the same page here, I'm afraid." Ava says. "Pun intended. But if you're interested, the more contemporary stuff is over here. Teens facing huge hurdles. Overcoming them. Lots of beautiful, important stuff written in just the last few years."

"None of those characters—no *book*—is going to help me feel better about—things," Mei says. Ava gives Mei her sad smile and I suddenly wish she would adopt all of us and take us home like the lost boys at the end of Peter Pan. The lost girls.

"Maybe not. But it's good company, isn't it? To know you're not alone?"

"Like the moon," I say.

"What?"

"Something my dad told me once."

The elephant was in the room anyway, wasn't it? Sitting right in the middle of our little huddle, coloring everything, even a conversation about books, with shades of gray, tinges of darkness.

"How are you, girls?" Ava asks.

"Not great," Brynn says. I'm not even that surprised that Brynn is the one to speak up first. And anyway, Ava makes everyone feel like she's known them for years and years, maybe even in a previous life. I used to believe that this was the mark of an empath, the imprint of her old soul. I don't know about any of that anymore, but I do hope that someday people will feel comforted by me the way that I do when I'm with her. "Just trying to cope."

"Me too," Ava answers.

"You too? Like the same as us, 'me too'?" Brynn asks.

"Mhmm."

"I'm so sorry."

"Do you mind if I ask — when?" Chloe asks.

"High school. Same as you."

"A teacher?"

"No," she says quietly. "It was a friend."

"Why didn't you tell me?" I ask. "All this time and you never...and I kept asking. I knew *something*..."

She comes over and presses her body against mine so that I'm swallowed up in her long violet sweater. Ava holds me close. The purple of her sweater collides with the thick black of my coat.

"I thought I could protect you. That if I could keep *you* close, it would make up for me not speaking up about what happened to me."

"It's everywhere."

"It is," Ava says. "Across cultures. Generations. In this town. In others."

"If I don't... turn him in... then I'm just as bad as him. I'm him."

"I love you," Ava says. "Always remember that. Okay? You're not him."

"You are not him, Charley," Brynn repeats quickly. "You're not him."

The girls come nearer. The world is very small. The books are close, like friends. The books, the girls, Ava: these are my anchors. These are the things I am meant to hold on to.

"This can't happen to anyone else ever again," Brynn says. "Not one more."

And she's right. She's absolutely right.

Not. One. More.

•   •   •

Dad's in the living room when I get home. He's staring at the TV, which is muted, the closed captioning on. This is how he always watches TV. He says he likes to exercise his brain a little.

I walk right past the flat screen and head for the stairs.

"You're not even going to say hello? Charley, can we talk for a second, please?"

This must be how Brynn feels when she's having one of her panic attacks. The walls close in on me, and like I'm looking through the viewfinder on mom's fancy camera, my vison narrows and all I see is him. There are no walls, no TV, no pillows, just him.

"Are you angry with me about something? Can we talk about it a little?"

It would be easier, it would be so much easier, if he was a tyrant, a crazy person, throwing me into walls, doing something, doing *anything* that would tell me that Brynn and Mei and Chloe are telling me the truth. But I have no facts; I have no evidence beyond their words. Is that enough? Can it be enough?

"Have I done something to upset you?"

"You—are—a very bad man," I choke out.

Because, *yes,* I decide. I trust my gut and I trust my friends. This is for all the children, the ones I know and those I've never even met, who haven't even been born yet, but who will, someday, someday, burst into this sick world and be asked to keep a secret. This, right now, is for every single girl or boy who has ever had a secret that sears a hole in their soul.

"What are you talking about? Come sit down, please."

There isn't even a trace of fear in his voice. Nothing! He doesn't believe his own daughter will out him. But I won't be on the wrong side of history anymore, denying truths just because they're too difficult to hear.

I don't sit down.

"Did you touch Brynn?"

And there it is. A pause in the air. A twitch of his eye, then a glance downward, before meeting my gaze again. It's nothing, maybe, but it's also everything.

I sink onto the steps.

I've never had a dad.

"What do you mean, Charley?" He regains his composure as quickly as he loses it.

"The moon... the blackbird..." I sputter. "When I was a little kid... you'd been having a fight that day with mom. Is that because she knows, too? Why does everyone know and no one says anything? Why does everyone protect you?"

"Who's everyone? What are you talking about?"

"Brynn. Chloe. Mei."

His face drains of color.

"And how many others? There must be more."

"Please," he says.

A key turns in the lock and Mom comes in, wearing scrubs beneath a thick coat. She takes one look at us and sits down next to me on the stairs. He's the one near tears, but she chooses to sit next to me instead.

"What in the world is going on here?" she asks me.

"I know I need to get help. And I will," Dad says. "But please don't tell anyone."

I see us. I see *us*—Dad, pushing me on a swing toward the expanse of sky. The books, so many of them, piled up beside us, me on his lap, asking for one more, just one more. *My little Bronte,* he would say. *My little bookworm.* I want to assure him. I want to say, *it's going to be okay, Dad,* just as he'd done for me when I'd left Bear at Grandma's house. But my voice finally cracking, I say, "This is for Brynn and Chloe and Mei and —-Ava."

"Oh." Mom puts her arms around my shoulders. It's the first time she's ever done so. I think it's the first time.

"Please," Dad says.

"Brynn. Chloe. Mei. Ava."

Feeling the strength of my mom's hands on me, I say their names again. And then I say them again. I just keep saying their names.

ꓮRYNN

All eyes are on me as I stand near the piano. I hold my music binder to my chest like it's a shield and I'm being attacked by an enemy's sword. I know I don't need to look at the lyrics and that my Catholic school training has been leading me up to this moment since day one, but I hold it, anyway.

Singing in the shower hasn't prepared me for this. If I could pick up my bathtub and stick it down on stage with me, I could definitely go on a national tour. But obviously, there's no steam and no soap and no gush of hot water on my hair right now, though I do feel just as naked.

Mrs. Miller hits the chord and I start to sing.

Ava Maria

Gratia plena

I'm barely making a sound. Abort! Cancel the tour. Refund the tickets. I make eye contact with Charley and Joss. They both nod at the same time. *Keep going. You've got this.*

I do *not* have it, definitely not, but I keep going.

Maria, gratia plena

Maria, gratia plena

I'm not Khadija. I'll never be Khadija, with her super mature voice and perfect posture, but I can't help but notice that a few of the chorus girls are looking at me a little differently than they were a minute ago. Chloe and Mei give me a thumbs-up.

I try to sing a little louder.

Emma cocks her head to the side and leans in, like she's trying to hear me better. Emma wants to hear *me*? Boring old me?

Ave, ave dominus

Dominus tecum

I start to cry. I don't know why it is that right now, when I'm trying to do this *thing*, this very scary thing, that my body has betrayed me. Judas tears. Maybe all the famous singers are really thinking about Judas when they audition. That's probably the key to nailing it. I could write a book about this technique.

The tears don't stop. Something about singing like this with the breath coming deep from my stomach is making me feel so open—vulnerable—in touch with everything going on around me. I feel the deep shame of Mr. Foster's fingers on my zipper, and Charley's fear. I remember the ice cream shop and the bookstore and Ava's violet sweater. I think of Mommy and the rituals that may or may not have saved her. Even though my parents don't know that

I'm auditioning, I feel their support and love from across streets and towns and through buildings.

I feel everything.

Benedicta tu in mulieribus

I sing through my tears. I don't stop, even when I can barely squeak the words out anymore. When I finally finish, there are six hundred years of silence — or — probably just a few seconds. Then my classmates clap. It's not just Charley and not just Joss and Chloe and Mei, but all of them, all of them: Emma, too, Khadija, too.

"Looks like we've found our soloist," Mrs. Miller says.

I legitimately think she's talking about Khadija, but everyone's looking at me and clapping, and suddenly I understand. *Me.* Mrs. Miller picked me.

"Your soul was in there. Thank you for being brave enough to share it with us."

I give a little nod and I know I'm totally awkward, classic, Brynn, but somehow, that's enough.

"We'll have to work on your volume a little. But if you want the solo, it's yours."

"Okay," I say. "Yes, I want it." My words are all slow and stupid, but I don't care. I really don't. I stumble back up to the riser next to Charley and Joss. "Thank you!" I remember to call out.

My classmates laugh, but I don't think they're being mean. I decide here and now: there's no such thing as a skein of fools.

"I knew you could do it!" Charley says.

Joss gives me a high-five.

It's the greatest day of my life.

•　　•　　•

I'm bursting.

Mommy and Daddy are acting totally normal, passing the asparagus around the dinner table and talking about work. They don't know that I'm about to explode and turn into a pile of Brynn dust. Except instead of ash, the dust will be sparkly with chunks of rhinestones.

I can't wait a second longer.

"I got it," I say, and wait. I want them to guess. Have a little fun.

"Got what?" Daddy raises one eyebrow. I don't know how he even does that. I used to try it when I was little by practicing in the mirror, but my eyebrows refused to be separated. Whatever one does, the other follows.

"Guess."

"SAT score?" Mommy says.

That's a buzz kill, right there.

"You got your *Macbeth* paper back?"

My stomach feels like it's been drop-kicked. I don't want to talk about that essay. Not now.

"The solo. I got the solo!"

My parents take exactly one second to register the information before they freak out. Daddy puts his fork down on his plate and Mommy jumps up from her chair and comes around to hug me.

"You did what? You got what?" She throws her arms around me. "You auditioned?"

"The winter concert solo?" Daddy asks. His eyes are lit up beneath those eyebrows, which are now both raised up toward his hairline.

"Brynn," Mommy says. She's crying. Maybe that's where I get my tearing-up on a dime thing from. Bad genes. "We are so, so, exceptionally proud of you."

"For getting it, of course, but mostly for trying. We know how much courage it had to take for you to audition."

"But it helps that I got it, right?"

Daddy and Mommy laugh and Mommy goes to sit back down across from me. She wipes her eyes with a napkin and then crumples it into a little ball.

"What made you decide to go for it?"

"I don't know. Charley said I have a nice voice."

"We've been telling you that for years."

"Singing in the shower doesn't exactly count."

"I understand," Daddy says. "I do. You needed to hear it from your friend."

"Charley, Charley, Charley," Mommy says. "She's such a mystery to me. But today I'm very grateful to her."

"A mystery?"

"A little offbeat, I mean."

I feel wildly defensive, like there's a guard dog clawing its way out of my chest.

"She's going through a lot. Just because she's not Catholic or whatever —"

"This has nothing to do with religion. I just think she maybe has had a lot to deal with during her very young life, and that the way she handles it is to daydream, or to come up with realities different from her own. Do you understand what I mean? I'm not sure her family is there for her the way that yours is for you."

"Your support and love and everything is amazing. But bad stuff has happened to me, too."

"What kind of bad stuff?" Daddy perks up. Oh, good Lord. He's therapying me again.

"Umm… Mommy had cancer." I point my fork at her.

"We got through that together. Right?" Mommy says.

"Yes, but like, you can't protect me from feeling of all of that."

Here come the waterworks. I grab for Mommy's balled up napkin. Might as well make it the official crying napkin of the evening. "There have been bad things that have happened to me that you don't even know about."

"Like what? What bad things?"

Everything else until now: the rituals, Joss's plan, all of that magic — those were just a fancy way of hiding out while we tried to convince ourselves that we were taking some kind of action.

This is the year we rise, Charley had said.

How?

This is how. This:

"I was assaulted at school. Two weeks ago. A teacher."

My parents stare at me. I stare at them.

"Oh my God," Mommy whispers. She gets up, just like she had a few minutes ago, and holds me in her arms like I'm a little baby, her little baby. And you know what? I am. I'm hers. And I'm Daddy's. But I'm mine, too. Just plain old me, belonging to no one.

"Do you want to talk about it?"

"I do. I mean- I will. But maybe… not right now?"

"Whenever you're ready. Any time at all."

"Police," Daddy says quietly.

"Yes. The police… when you're ready," Mommy says again.

I take another deep breath. I won't let the panic get me now. Not when I've come so far.

"I'm ready."

Mommy hugs me even harder, if that's possible. And I know—I understand—that she's forgiven me for the time I asked her why she didn't get that mastectomy. She loves me with her whole heart. Her giant ambassador heart. She would walk the world over for me. I would walk the world for her.

I should have told her about Mr. Foster sooner. But I also understand why I didn't. I forgive myself for that. And at least I've told her now. She lets go of me and brings our plates over to the counter. None of us are hungry anymore.

Once the dishes are cleared and the uneaten food put away, we settle onto the couch together and put on a silly movie. Willow walks back and forth between our laps and we try to laugh at him, though it's not exactly funny. It's very awkward and I'm completely uncomfortable with all of this weird information hanging between us, but I also feel so much lighter. That secret was weighing me down.

I lean my head on Daddy's shoulder, and he kisses my hair.

CHARLEY

I guess I thought there were going to be jail cells. Men, women, deranged, screaming, gesturing to us to come closer, a little closer, while an officer bangs on the bar with her baton. But the station is nothing like that. The front room is bare and quiet, with two officers sitting at a long reception desk. Behind them, through glass doors, a dozen tables face one another, computers and printers arranged around the room just like in our lab at school.

They're all here. Mei with her mom, Joss with her dad, Chloe and Brynn, each with both of their parents. I came alone.

Some of us sit, waiting, in a few scattered aluminum chairs. Mei and Joss stand off to the side, near a greasy window with a few cutout snowflakes and a sad string of large colored bulbs. I'm on the floor, at Brynn's feet. She gives me a massage while her dad is at the reception desk.

"We'd like to file a report," Mr. McLaughlin says.

"Who would?"

"All of us."

"*All* of you?"

"Yes," Mei and Joss say together.

"Four of the girls. One of them is here for support."

"We'll have to do this one at a time."

"That's fine."

"Whoever's first can follow Officer Stephens, then."

A quick look around, but we all know it's Brynn. It's Brynn who has to be first. She and her mom stand up and join Mr. McLaughlin. We jump up and swarm over to her, enclosing her up in a hug.

"You've got this," Chloe says. "We believe in you."

"Thank you for being here," Brynn says to me. "Charley, it just means everything."

Joss squeezes my hand as Brynn and her parents are led to an unmarked private office in the corner that I didn't see was there until now.

"Are you okay?" Joss whispers.

And I'm small. And I'm scared. And I'm sick.

But I'm also okay. I'm also strong.

My power, my sense of righteousness, my belief in friendship, grows every day.

"Is this hard?" Mei asks.

"It's time," I say.

• • •

Three police officers take him while he's in the middle of the hall. He holds *Macbeth* and his sagging orange lunch bag. He wears his reading glasses, a green pen tucked behind his ear. Our principal, Ms. Suarez, stands nearby. All movement stops.

You have the right to remain silent.

"Don't watch, Charley." It's Emma who says this. It's Khadija who pulls on my arm. A hundred silent things pass between us. Forgiveness. Understanding. And empathy. Of all things, empathy. "I'm so sorry you have to be here for this. Please don't look."

But I do watch, even though I already know it's a thing I'll never unsee.

Anything you say can and will be used against you in a court of law.

They cuff him. I hear the click, even here, from down the hall. He doesn't look up from the ground. We don't look at each other, which is fine. I don't really want to see into his eyes, anyway. Who knows what I'll find there?

The police lead him out. A freshman girl cries, which is really just ridiculous. Who are you? Why are you crying? The hallway erupts into whispers and then nudges and everyone stares at me. Same as all the elementary school birthday parties, same as the skating rink. Except maybe not the same.

Maybe not the same at all. "I'm sorry, Charley," Julian whispers.

Principal Suarez follows my classmates' eyes, rushes down the hall to me, and then locks me up in her arms, directing me toward the stairwell.

We push through the double doors to the stairs and I collapse onto the bottom one while Ms. Suarez stands over me and I stare at my new boots. The toes are already worn.

"You're shaking."

"So are you," I say.

"Yes, you're right; I am," she whispers. "Charley, did you know?"

"Didn't you?"

"I had hoped—I had chosen —"

But she doesn't need to finish that sentence and she knows it. She's guilty, too. As guilty as the rest of us. As guilty as us all.

•   •   •

Mom is on the phone for hours. Lawyers, mostly, but also a few relatives. She talks about bail, which makes me feel sick.

When she finally gets off of the phone, she joins me in the living room. She's straight from the overnight shift and smells of baby powder and blankets and warm, good things. Mom sits next to me. There's still a stack of Dad's colored pens on the coffee table.

"How are you?" Mom asks.

This question coming from her is both new and impossible to answer.

"Everything hurts." I decide to test it out. "Like my body is on fire or something." A toe in the water. If Mom passes, I'll say more. If she fails, I'll never have a serious conversation with her ever again.

"I think that's normal."

"Nothing about this is normal."

"I just meant... how you feel."

"Mom, did you know? This whole time?"

She sighs. It's a familiar sound, an anger that I grew up with and often ran away from.

"I suspected, I guess; though not to this extent. I didn't think—how could anyone possibly imagine that their husband —"

"Did you know about Ava?"

"Ava?"

"In high school. Something happened to her, too."

There's a sound from deep in mom's throat. Not words, just a low hum. The same low hum that's been an undercurrent to my entire life. There it was, ticking along, just underneath the surface, while we made pancakes and talked about the Bronte sisters. How stupid I was. How blind.

"Mom," I say. "Did. You. Know. About. Dad?"

"There were signs I brushed aside." Her eyes well up and I'm again filled with her anger, but something else, too. Something different. Regret.

Shame. "I thought... oh, I don't know. I thought the things that all women think."

"What do all women think? What do you mean?"

"Oh, Charley. Things that I hope you never feel about yourself. That you should *never* feel, because you're beautiful and bright and talented."

"And you're not?"

"I thought that maybe I was those things, but just not—*enough*."

Like flipping my blog posts, back through time, I remember that night, so long ago, with the slammed porch door and the lightning bugs and the dead bird and the moon—the silence mom left behind. She's been in constant pain, constant doubt, because of Dad, and I let him charm me with talk of the moon and books and poets.

"I'm sorry. I didn't understand." I look up at her. "Am I — am I enough? For you?"

"Always! Always, always."

"And you are enough for me. Actually, not even just for me. You are enough, Mom."

"Thank you, Charley."

"Do you think we can... start over? Somehow?"

"Do you even want to? I have failed you in every conceivable way."

"I think maybe—he did."

"When did you get so smart? So much wiser than me."

I take a deep breath, prepared to wade further into the pond.

"I *feel* things," I whisper. "The things that I feel make me know about how the world works and how... people work."

"What, like magic?" Mom laughs a little through her tears.

"I used to think so, but now I'm not sure."

"Like what, then?"

I think of my lonely walk home and the way Ava had picked me up and held me close. I see her violet sweater. I hear Brynn singing and Joss and Mei and Chloe's laughter at the ice cream shop, where the hundreds of flavors called to us beneath the counter. I see The Ravens, our circle, our feathers touching, one, two, three, four, five. But more truthfully, more importantly: I just see *us*. My friends.

I don't answer. Don't need to. Instead, I lean in and put my forehead on Mom's. She pulls me close.

•　　•　　•

In the safety of my room, with the purple light and the rows of books and the ceiling covered in stars, I throw myself on top of my bed with my tablet. I open a new draft on my blog and begin to type. I type like I'm running from something. I write like I'm trying to save my own life. And maybe I am. Maybe I am.

I know this blog has been quiet for some time now. Thank you for being patient with me while I figured some things out. The truth is, I was ready to give it all up. I was ready to throw it all away. But I've had a lot of time to think. And during that time, I reflected on magic and spells and rituals, of course, but also on love and friendship and the meaning of loyalty.

Maybe I don't need a Circle to have friends. Maybe genuine friendship is as simple as saying, "I believe you." It is as ordinary and as uncommon, as easy and as difficult as raising our voices together in the name of justice. But standing together is how we win. Standing together is how we rise.

I hit publish without re-reading and toss the tablet onto my nightstand. It's time to get ready for the concert with my friends. I get up and pull my dress out of my backpack. It needs to be ironed. I'll have to hurry. Not much time now.

I race out of my bedroom and toward the linen closet. Maybe I'm not running away from something after all. Maybe I'm running *toward* something, I think, as I plug the iron into the wall. I've never needed a boy to kiss me. I've never wanted a girl to like me like "that." Maybe I never will, not ever, in this life. Instead, I'm going to race back to school, where I'll join my friends in the locker room. We'll sing together, our voices raised and aligned, their energy and love all bound up in mine. Because after all that, after everything: Magic is as easy as letting love inside.

ⒷRYNN

We break our rule and take a selfie in the locker room.

Joss has the longest arms, so she holds the phone and we all squish in front of it. Our matching blue dresses crash into each other. The blue sparkles get all mixed up together until we can't even tell whose dress is whose.

"Say *Ave Maria*," Joss says, and that makes me laugh, so my eyes are closed in our one and only selfie. It's okay. I think there'll be more.

"Charley just popped her selfie cherry." A bunch of girls hear her and laugh too and we fill the locker room with giggling and nervous talking and bursts of song and flashes of iridescent blue.

"Ew!" Charley says, but she doesn't seem angry the way she sometimes is when Joss talks about that kind of stuff. Then she turns to me. "Are you ready?"

I hear the audience out in the auditorium. They're seated already. I imagine Mommy and Daddy are in the front row with their smiles big and bright. Mommy already told me she put two packages of tissues in her purse because she plans on crying the entire concert. I hope I don't disappoint her, because I haven't yet figured out the logistics of singing while puking.

"Nauseous," I say. "Maybe Khadija should just —"

"Nope," Charley and Joss say at the same time.

The locker room door opens and Mrs. Miller comes in. We must be starting soon. I sit down on the bench and all the girls gather round to hear Mrs. Miller's final announcement.

"We're about ready to take your places," she says. "How are you all feeling? Brynn?"

"She's fine," Chloe says.

"Ummm —"

But Joss interrupts me. "Totally fine."

"Good," Mrs. Miller says. "Ready for our moment of silence?"

Before every concert, we all gather before getting on stage and take a minute to breathe and center ourselves. Mrs. Miller says it's the key for all kinds of performers: singers, actors, even gymnasts and ice skaters.

"Yes," Joss says, but a few girls look at each other and dash off to the lockers or to their backpacks, which are thrown all over the place like the locker room threw up instead of me.

"Just a sec!" Emma says. Only Charley, Joss and I stay with Mrs. Miller. We watch everyone else, even Chloe and Mei, scatter, like they're on some kind of secret mission.

"What are you doing?" Mrs. Miller asks, as they come back again, all holding something behind their backs.

"We're ready now," Chloe says.

"Okay, then... let's take a moment in silence together."

I don't know what they're doing. I don't know why we weren't included—but I trust them. I bow my head and the locker room gets quiet.

I take a few deep breaths to settle my stomach. With my classmates all around me, with Mrs. Miller here and Joss and Charley so close, I let myself feel it. I give myself over to it: the pain, the grief, the shame, but also the joy, the wonder. The beauty of it all.

In another second, the moment is over, and we file out onto the stage. Joss and Charley stay close. The locker room door swings shut behind us.

•　　•　　•

The stage lights are bright and dazzling as we take our places out on the risers. We'll sing one song together and then it's my solo and after that, I'll finally be able to relax. The audience claps like crazy as we enter, and even though we all know it's just our parents out there, the clapping is nice.

Mrs. Miller plays and we sing.

Go, tell it on the mountain over the hills and everywhere

I know the song is about Christmas, but I can't help but feel that it's meant for me, too. *Go tell it, Brynn*, the song says. Your story is yours to share. Maybe someday, I'll shout it from the rooftops. Maybe someday, I'll use my story to help others who have gone through the same thing.

He made me a watchman
Upon a city wall

It feels good. It feels great to sing with everyone. But the song is finished too soon. The applause is over too quickly and suddenly, it's my turn. Charley squeezes my hand as everyone else sits down. I get up and adjust my dress. Everyone's eyes are on me as I make my way downstage to where the microphone sits in its stand. It's already adjusted to my height. It's ready and waiting.

I'm shaking. I'm shaking so hard that I can't imagine I'm going to be able to do this at all. I have the quick thought of running off of the stage and Khadija getting up to sing in my place. But the music is already starting. I clear my throat. I'm pretty sure that nothing is going to squeak out, when suddenly, from behind me, I sense movement rushing through the risers. What *is* that? What's happening? I know I shouldn't, but I turn around for a quick look.

Feathers.

Every single one of my classmates holds a black feather in front of them. Even Charley, even Joss. Chloe gets up from the riser and hands me one, too, and the piano stops. I take a moment to thank her, to thank all The Ravens with my eyes. I feel the presence of that same magical hand that told me what to say when the three of us were out on the bleachers that day. Maybe that hand is what Mommy calls God. Maybe it's what Charley calls energy. But whatever it is—I feel it. I'm part of it. I'm welcome.

I take a deep breath. There's no panic. There's only stillness. There's only sadness. There's only hope. Mrs. Miller looks up at us and at me. I give a small nod and she plays again.

Ave Maria, I begin.

My sound is small and slight as the tears roll down, and I smooth the feather between my fingers. I see Mommy and Daddy out there. They're in the front row, just as I thought they'd be. I see Ava and Malik and Leo stand and step into the side aisle with feathers in their hands, too. Mommy reaches for her tissues. My classmates stand behind me. They stand with me.

Gratia plena, I sing. I make my voice loud.

ACKNOWLEDGEMENTS

This book would not have been possible without my village. Thank you to Sarah L, my former and first agent, and my first professional champion. Thank you, Reagan R. and all the Black Rose Writing team, for your support and collaboration.

Thank you to my creative tribe: My Lady Friends, Jessica P., Lauri M., and Karen T., who daily listen and respond to all the unimportant things, which are, of course, in the end, the only things that really matter. Thank you to my earliest and most avid reader, my dear friend, Therese C., and also to Amanda E., who read and reread, even from afar. Thank you, Leah L., for giving me light; this book exists, in part, because of you. Thank you to all of my NJ Theatre Family; you are home.

Special thanks to my high school English teachers and both undergraduate and graduate school writing professors. I believe that most writers can speak of a cherished English teacher. I'm lucky enough to speak of many.

Thank you to my mother-in-law Barbara and my father-in-law, Keith, for watching the baby in the early days so that I could steal away and write. Thank you to my brother, Ryan, for the Instagram lessons. Thank you, Grandma, for being my first and most early advocate. I wish you were here to see this. Thank you to my mom, who said to always, always follow your instincts, even if these instincts are based on dreams.

And finally, thank you to my husband, Adam, who helped me carve out the time, never wavered in his support, and who always said, "someday."

ABOUT THE AUTHOR

Author photo courtesy of Lauren Beischer

Jackie received her MFA in Creative Writing from The New School and her BS in English Education from New York University. Aside from writing for young adults, she is also actively involved in theatre, and has acted and directed across the tri-state area. As a playwright, she's had work produced in both NYC and NJ. Jackie lives in NJ with her husband, two children, and (very handsome) golden retriever, Gatsby. This is her debut novel.

We hope you enjoyed reading this title from:

BLACK ROSE writing™

www.blackrosewriting.com

Subscribe to our mailing list—*The Rosevine*—and receive **FREE** books, daily deals, and stay current with news about upcoming releases and our hottest authors.

Scan the QR code below to sign up.

Already a subscriber? Please accept a sincere thank you for being a fan of Black Rose Writing authors.

View other Black Rose Writing titles at www.blackrosewriting.com/books and use promo code **PRINT** to receive a **20% discount** when purchasing.

2R00178